MOMMY POISONED OUR HOUSE GUEST

OR REALITY ACCORDING TO CB

by Shenan (CB) Leaver
with Betty Lou Leaver

Second edition.

ISBN 0-9679907-0-X

Authors: Shenan (CB) Leaver, Betty Lou Leaver
Cover design and interior graphics: Carl Leaver

MSI Press
784 Northridge PMB 293
Salinas, CA 93906
MSInt@AOL.COM
www.mindsolutionsinternational.com

Table of Contents

Hi, There!   ix

I Thank the People Who Helped Me   xi

Mommy's Domestic Disasters
Kitchen Chaos   3
Mommy's Cookies   7
Shopping Catastrophe   9
There is a Stranger in Mommy's Bed!   11
Our Poisoned Guest   13
Honored Guests   15
Painting Problem Solution   17
The Man in Our Dumpster   19

Mommy's Clothing Calamities
A Personalized View of San Francisco   23
In a Hurry   25
Escape from a Hungry Escalator   27
In Plain View   29
Casual Attire   31
That Doggone Skirt   33

Mommy's Missing Details
Raindrops Keep Falling on Her Head   37
The Babysitter   39
Things That Grow   41
A Missing Pigtail   43
The Empty Chair   45
Faulty Impressions   47

On the Road with Mommy

Those Darn Keys   53
The Car That Would Not Start   55
Maps in the Head   57
The Power of Observation   61
The Value of an Open Ear on the Open Road   63
The Three-Event Trip   67
The Driver   69
Driving the Big One   71
Washing Cars and Clothes, Needed or Not   73

Mommy's Transportation Tribulations

Trouble with Cars   77
More Trouble with Cars   79
Teaching My Sister to Drive
    while Cowering under the Seat   81
Trouble on Foot   83
All Aboard   85

Up in the Air and around the World with Mommy

A Questionable Heritage   89
Not a Terrorist   93
Ticket Trouble   95
Trouble with Travels   99
Fun with Luggage   103
Meeting People in Boston   105

Mommy on the Farm

Starting Young   109
Fishing for Men   111
A Farmer in Leningrad   113
The Driving Instructor   117
Red Snow   119

It Could Only Happen to Mommy

Lacking the Luck of Ganesha	123
My Mommy Wore Combat Boots	127
Mommy's Special Weapon	131
Thinking Literally	133
Typing Typos	135
Mommy and the Priest	137
Life in Cyberspace	139
Moldovan Roulette	141
The End	143
About the Authors	145

Shenan (CB) Leaver (with Betty Lou Leaver)

Hi, There!

Hi! My name is CB. At least, that is what everyone calls me. I do have another name. It is Shenan Carl Leaver, but almost no one calls me that.

Let me tell you a little bit about myself. I like to organize things and to manage what other people do. Most especially, I like to make plans. Mommy says that my favorite phrase is "I've got a plan!" Well, I've got a plan now. My plan is to tell you some stories about my mommy. She says they're embarrassing. Daddy says they're normal for Mommy. I say they're funny. You decide!

Now, let me tell you about my mommy. Perhaps you have met her—my mommy? She's like the lady next door, except that all kinds of strange and funny things happen to her. She rushes to the bus stop, ready to attack the workday with a vengeance—except that she seems to have forgotten something that leaves everyone staring. Airplanes fall apart on her, and road trips somehow end up in the wrong states. Then, when she is exhausted, she flops into bed and finds a "stranger" there.

Mommy says that there are two kinds of people: the detail-observant and the detail-oblivious. Some folks are detail-observant. They notice immediately if a neighbor has purchased a new truck, someone has rearranged the living room furniture, or the house is on fire. Other people don't seem to notice such "little" details—but they might notice a house on fire if it is their own and they are sitting in it and starting to feel hot. Mommy calls these people detail-oblivious.

My mommy is detail-oblivious. I like that because odd things happen to detail-oblivious people. Life with a detail-oblivious person can be a whole lot of fun.

This book contains only true stories about my mommy, but Mommy made me change the names of her friends (and her bosses). She says that I should protect the innocent—and her. I don't quite understand that because most all of the people I talk about in this book are guilty of the things I describe, including Mommy. Well, Mommy says that they have to be treated as if they are innocent. So, I did that.

I got the idea for this book from Jacqueline Reuss. She was my mommy's secretary, and she thought funny things happened to Mommy. She said that someone ought to write a book about Mommy. So, I did. Thank you, Jacqueline. That was a fun idea! We got you, Mommy!

I dedicate this book to Dr. Joan Landy, Karen Lindstrom, and Sue Scott, who were some of my teachers, and to Julie McGlinchey, my reading tutor. They all thought there was hope for me to become something called literate, but they were the only ones who thought so—except, of course, for my mommy, my relatives, and my family's friends. As for me, I'm starting to believe now.

I Thank the People Who Helped Me

I want to thank my mommy for doing funny things so that I could write about her. She also helped me with the writing, which is hard for me, but I am learning all the time to read and write better.

I also want to thank my daddy for typesetting the book; that means, he put the pages together on the computer and made this a real book. He also put in the funny pictures. Most important, he made the funny covers for both the first and seccond editions of this book (This one you are reading is the second edition). Thank you, Daddy.

Some people who read better than I do read the prepublication version of the first edition of this book and pointed out things I could write better. So, I want to thank Diane Bolduc, Dave Bear and Di Edgerly, David Halbeisen, Erica Ham, Jacqueline Reuss, Donna Smith, and Julie Trudell for their help. Also, Kevin Ham, when he read the first version, gave Mommy a good idea for improving the description of what happened to Mommy in "Shopping Catastrophe."

A very warm thank-you goes to all the people who read the first edition of my book, especially to those who read it and liked it! A lot (or maybe most) of them I don't know personally, but if they liked the first edition of this book, I bet we could become friends!

I always give a copy of my book to anyone who comes to visit Mommy. I think they should know about Mommy, and I want to make them laugh, which they always do, when they read the stories. Mommy is not always happy when I do that, though, because sometimes her guests get scared. They don't want to stay to dinner. I don't think that is so bad. They always suggest taking her and Daddy to dinner some place else. (Better than Mommy's cooking!)

I especially want to thank my reading teacher, Julie. She thought that writing this book was a great idea. She read some of the stories before I finished the whole first edition of this book. She said I should be proud. I am. I hope she is proud, too.

MOMMY'S DOMESTIC DISASTERS

Shenan (CB) Leaver (with Betty Lou Leaver)

Kitchen Chaos

My mommy is a very nice mommy, but she is a very bad cook. When my sister needed to take some deviled eggs to Rainbow Girls' meeting, my mommy made them. Mommy didn't really want to make them. She wanted to find some place to buy them. However, the leader of the Rainbobw Girls' chapter told Mommy that they were asking all the mommies to make, not buy, the food contributions in order to set a good example for the girls in the chapter. Some example!

Aginst her better judgment and protesting all the way, my sister, Fawn, took them to her meeting. We all knew what would happen. Sure enough, Fawn came back home with all the eggs except one. After one person had tasted one of the eggs, no one else wanted to eat them. Mommy said she did not understand what the problem was. She had made only one small change to the recipe. Since she did not have any paprika, she used something that she thought would be okay because it looked very much like paprika: cayenne pepper.

That's how my mommy cooks, and I guess that's how she always cooked. When she was a little girl, she cooked a cake for Grandpa. He did not like it. He said it was not fit for the pigs, and he threw it into the pigpen. Mommy was very unhappy. The pigs would not eat her cake, and every day when she slopped the pigs, she saw the cake sitting in the corner of the pigpen where the pigs had pushed it away. I guess at some point, it just disappeared because it was something called biodegradable. At least, that's what I think happened because years later when I stayed on Grandma's farm, I fell into the pigpen, and the cake was gone.

Mommy was very disappointed in Grandpa—and in the pigs. She thought maybe her friends would appreciate her cooking better than they do. So, she made another cake. Grandpa's cake had been a spice cake, and Mommy had put in every spice in the cupboard (after all, it said to spice to test and she liked all the spices she had put in) to make sure she had all the ones that Grandpa liked. This time, Mommy decided to make just a plain old pound cake, but, of course, being rather creative by nature, she added her own touches to it. The cake turned out rather nicely—or so she thought. She took it to school and offered it to the cafeteria lady (believe it or not, the school actually let Mommy work in the cafeteria—but, of course, they did not let her cook). The cafeteria lady tested it. Yes! It was edible! So, she but it into pieces and put it out for the students to try, but nobody wanted any at all. All the pieces were still there when lunch was over. The cafeteria lady told Mommy that the students probably did not like Mommy's innovation with food coloring. Most people aren't eager to eat a cake that is green on the inside.

That's why we don't let Mommy cook! Mommy used to scare us. She told us that if we did not help clean up the house, she would cook supper. We really hurried and worked hard to get everything cleaned fast, so that Daddy would cook supper.

We learned to cook, too. I like the way my brother and sisters cook better than the way Mommy cooks. Mommy got mad about that once, though. She had an important visitor. My brother, who was twelve years old at that time, made pot roast for dinner. It was very good. Mommy was very pleased with him until the guest complimented him on his cooking, and he said. "Thank you, but in this house, knowing how to cook is self-defense."

My mommy's secretary, Jacqueline, was a good cook, though. So, once when it was my birthday, I called her and asked her to make my birthday cake. She said she could not because

4

she would not be home that evening. I cried really hard. I told her that if she did not make my cake, Mommy would! So, Jacqueline told Mommy to buy me a cake. (Whew!)

Every once in a while, though, Mommy thinks that it is okay for her to cook. Once she decided to have a BBQ for all the people who worked for her. That was a good decision, and it should have been and actually was a lot of fun. She also decided that she would like to make braided bread for the BBQ. That was not a good decision, but it was fun. She made the dough, put it in a bowl to rise, and then became involved in other things until it was be time to braid the bread and bake it. While Mommy was working on other things, the doorbell rang. It was her secretary, Irene, who had come early to see if she could help with anything. Mommy thanked her and assured her that everything was under control. Irene did not believe her, though, because she could see some white stuff oozing out the kitchen door into the living room. It was Mommy's dough! She had left it for too long, and it had risen up and out of the bowl, down the stove, and across the floor. Who knows where it would have run off to had Irene not shown up when she did?

Daddy lets Mommy cook Christmas dinner. I keep telling him not to, but lots of times it has turned out okay. Each time that was a very pleasant surprise. However, last year, it happened! I knew it would. Mommy burned the ham. We could not eat it; there was only a black outside shell—all the inside had burned away. No stores were open, so we all went to a restaurant for Christmas dinner. What can I say? I told Daddy not to let Mommy cook!

Conclusion:
Just putting on an apron does not make anyone a cook!

Shenan (CB) Leaver (with Betty Lou Leaver)

Mommy's Cookies

One thing Mommy can usually cook okay is cookies. They are not special in any way, but they are usually edible. Actually, when Mommy was a little girl, she won a cooking contest for cookies. She made rainbow cookies: the dough was all kinds of colors mixed together. Mommy also made a big chart with the ingredients. On the chart, she made a writing mistake. Instead of baking powder, she wrote baking *power*. The judges thought that was funny. Mommy won an award for originality in cooking, but she said that she never figured out whether the originality was for the rainbow colors or for the power that she put into her baking ingredients.

Sometimes when the school had a bake sale, Mommy made cookies. People who bought them probably should have tasted them first. Mommy said that it did not matter. She said that people did not necessarily buy the cookies to eat them; they bought them to help the school. So, every time there was a PTA bake sale, Mommy would get busy making cookies, and we would all stay very far away from the kitchen, in case she wanted us to taste them.

Once my mommy made some cookies the evening before a bake sale for the school band. She wrapped the plate of cookies in saran wrap and put it on the counter.

The next morning my sister, Echo, took the plate to the car and handed it to my mommy. We lived too far from the high school for Echo to walk to school with all her books and band instruments, but we lived officially too close for her to be bussed. So, Mommy drove her to school every morning. The rest of us got to go along for the ride. That was fun because we drove through our neighborhood and often saw people we knew.

On the cookie day, our neighbors were especially friendly. Every time we stopped at a stop sign or a light, people waved at us very energetically. We all waved back and smiled. Even people we did not know waved enthusiastically. Some of the pointed toward the sky; we did that, too. It was a nice, sunny day. We liked the sky that day, too. We sure lived in a friendly town with nice weather.

When we got to school, Mommy got out of the car. As she stood up, she saw the roof of the car. On the top of the roof, held in place by the saran wrap, was the plate of cookies. Now we knew why all those people were waving and pointing so wildly.

Conclusion:
Saran wrap is fantastic stuff!

Shopping Catastrophe

Mommy does not like to shop, but she does go shopping sometimes. It is probably good that she does not go shopping too often. The times that she does are interesting. If it were more frequently, it might be irritating—or worse. Let me give you an example.

Once my mommy and her friend, Zitta, went grocery shopping. At that time, Zitta and her daughter, Yuliya, were living with us.

Zitta is like my mommy in many ways. Like my mommy, she does not see details. In the case of food, people like Zitta and Mommy do not see apples and oranges. Instead, they see fruit.

Anyway, Mommy and Zitta came home from the store with a lot of food, but it was not the kind of food we usually eat. In fact, I did not even know what some of the food was.

My sister, Echo, was quite surprised at the food she saw on the kitchen counter. There were spicy chicken livers, cow tongue, and tripe. I did not know what those things were, but Echo did and really hoped that Mommy was not going to make us eat that stuff. There also was more unrecognizable food: green mealy stuff, gloppy blue stuff (maybe it was for cleaning and not for eating), grey-colored bread, and some bright orange skinny things that looked like vegetables but certainly weren't carrots. Yuck!. Echo went to find Mommy to ask what all these colorful foods were. More important, she wanted to know why Mommy had bought them.

Mommy did not know what all those strange things were, either!, By way of explanation, she said, "Aunt Zitta put them in the basket, so I bought them. Frankly, I have no idea what all that stuff is. I just figured Aunt Zitta wanted it."

Meanwhile, Yuliyahad seen the strange food, too, and was equally surprised by it. So, she asked Zitta what the food was and why she and Mommy had bought it. She got a surprising answer.

Zitta said, "Aunt Betty Lou put it in the basket, so I said nothing. Frankly, I have no idea what it is. I just figured she wanted it."

Echo and Yuliya then confronted their mothers with their near identical answers. It turns out that neither had put the food in question into the basket. In fact, neither remembered taking a basket at the door. So, obviously, they had waltzed off with someone else's grocery cart and bought someone else's food.

I have always wondered what happened to the person who had collected all that weird food. I especially wonder how long it took for that person to stop looking for the missing cart and start shopping all over again. Poor person—it is not always good luck to run into Mommy!

Conclusion:
Do not send someonewho does not see the difference
between apples and oranges to the store.

There is a Stranger in Mommy's Bed!

Sometimes Mommy gets really tired. She says that working mothers reach proportions of exhaustion that exceed the imagination. In such cases, what they say and do have little resemblance to common sense. I guess that must be right, if I judge by my mommy.

For example, let me tell you what happened to her one weekend. Friday evening after a long and frustrating, to say nothing of exhausting, week at work, she fell asleep on the living room sofa. (She does that a lot. She says she is going to watch television, but she never does. She just stares at the screen for a few minutes and then topples over. I have never seen her watch a whole television show, like my siblings and I do.)

Anyway, she did her frequent act of screen staring and toppling over on the Friday evening I am talking about. My daddy, of course, could not wake her up; he never can when she topples over asleep. So, my sister found her asleep on the couch on Saturday morning.

"Mom, wake up!" she said.

"Huh?" Mommy struggled to bring herself back into the world of the living. It really is not very easy to wake up Mommy.

"Mom, Mom! You're on the couch! Why aren't you in bed?"

Mommy tried groggily to recall where she was and why.

"Oh, because when I tried to go to bed, there was someone in my bed," Mommy mumbled and turned over to go back to sleep.

That was a scary thought! My sister crept cautiously into Mommy's bedroom to see who or what was in the bed.

"Mom, Mom!" My sister had come back and was shaking Mommy, trying to get her to wake up. It is very, very hard to wake up Mommy.

"That's Dad in the bed!" my sister told her.

"Oh," Mommy mumbled and turned over to go back to sleep again.

"Mom," my sister asked with a tone of great surprise. "If you thought there was a stranger in your bed, why didn't you call the police, instead of just simply choosing another place to sleep?"

Conclusion:
When you are tired, you may not see things as they really are.

Our Poisoned Guest

Once a friend of Mommy's came to visit. His name was Steve, and he and Mommy were writing a book together.

Mommy decided that Steve would sleep in one of our guestrooms. However, that particular room had a nearby bathroom that had not been used in a long time, and the toilet was discolored. Mommy asked a friend who knows a lot about taking care of houses what she should do. The friend told her that Clorox would turn the toilet white again. Mommy was very happy. She bought a jug of Clorox.

When Steve arrived, he wanted to use the bathroom. Mommy proudly showed him the sparkling clean bathroom.

Steve went into the bathroom for a few minutes. Then we heard two loud sounds, one right after the other. Slam! Slam! The first slam was the bathroom door, and the second slam was the door to the outdoors. Steve streaked past us, screaming. His words started out loud, then in a Doppler effect, got quieter as he dashed past us, down the stairs, and into the streets, "It's a goddam gas chamber in there!"

Mommy's friend had not told Mommy to use only a little bit of Clorox, so she used the entire two-gallon jug. Poor Mommy!

Mommy forgot to flush the Clorox away before Steve came, so when he flushed the toilet after using it, the whole room filled with Clorox bubbles, just like in a real gas chamber. Poor Steve!

After that, Steve started calling Mommy "Little Miss Homemaker." It sounded like a compliment, but Mommy said that Steve did not mean it that way.

I guess that means that Mommy will not be selected as Homemaker of the Year this year. Poor Mommy!

Conclusion:
Not everyone can be Homemaker of the Year!

Honored Guests

Sometimes people called bigwigs visit Mommy. Usually these are very nice people, and they look just like my friends and me, only bigger. So I know why they are called big. Most, however, have very nice hair. In fact, none of them, as far as I can tell, wear wigs. (At least, I'm pretty sure they don't because I pulled one's hair once, and the hair stayed on his head.) Oh, well, maybe they just wear their big wigs on special occasions. I keep hoping to see them sometime, though, since other people seem to think they are pretty special things.

My brother says my mommy is not a very good entertainer because she has not bought much furniture. I guess he thinks that bigwigs need special chairs. Perhaps they do if they have their wigs on, but when they are with us—without their wigs—they seem to fit into our chairs just fine.

I will give you an example. On one occasion, Mommy entertained several bigwigs—all without their wigs. They sat around our dining room table on the fun chairs that my brothers and sisters and I use.

One settled into a desk chair that we rolled in from the office. (Mommy moves furniture from one place to another all the time; she calls it all-purpose furniture.) This bigwig must have been having a fun time with our desk chair because he kept rolling up to and away from the table. Mommy did not say anything to him about this bad behavior. That was unfair. She never lets me play that way.

Bigwig #2 sat in one of our lawn chairs. The chair was low, and the table was high. His chin was at the level of the table. My brother thought he should have some pillows, but our guest said he was okay. Clearly, he was. His mouth was closer to his plate than anyone else's was. That meant that it would be easier not to spill food so that Mommy would not get mad at him.

Bigwig #3 perched on top of my old, rickety high chair. It's so old that it is called an "anteek." It is a neat chair because it wobbles in lots of fun ways. Sometimes if you get it wobbling fast enough, it tips over. Wheee! Mommy does not like that. She does not let me sit on the high chair anymore. I do not think it is fair that she let our guest sit there. Fair or not, I tried to be nice. I pushed the high chair so that he could see how much fun the wobble was. That did not make Mommy happy. I guess my brother is right. She does not know how to entertain guests well.

Conclusion:
Bigwigs without their wigs are just like you and me.

Painting Problem Solution

Mommy says that she likes to paint, but sometimes I wonder if she really does. Maybe it is not that she likes to paint but rather than she likes to have things painted.

One time, when we were to have someone named Vanessa staying with us for a while, Mommy decided to paint Vanessa's room herself. She wanted it to be clean and pretty.

Mommy knew what was needed. She bought the right kinds of paintbrushes, enough white paint for the whole room, and a large, plastic drop cloth. She was ready.

Mommy carefully covered the green carpet with the drop cloth. Then she shook and poured out the paint. Now she was really ready!

Mommy quickly put a lot of paint on the walls. Mommy usually works very fast. However, she always misses details, and this time was no exception. As she painted, she kept moving closer and closer to where she had placed the paint pan. That made her work go faster and faster. Soon Mommy had painted almost all of the room.

She backed up to see how much she had completed and how much more she had to do. As she backed up, she stepped into the paint pan. Oh, no!

Mommy was very frustrated. She had white paint all over her feet. She comforted herself with the fact that at least she had not spilled the paint when she stepped into the paint pan. She bent over to pick up the paint pan, but her feet were slippery from the paint. She fell down, ripped the drop cloth, and knocked over the paint pan. Now the carpet and Mommy were the same color as the walls!

Well, Mommy gave up about the same time that Vanessa showed up. Vanessa offered to finish painting, and she did a very good job. She did not step into the paint pan. Mommy came to watch and was very pleased with how Vanessa was painting.

Tom Sawyer liked to paint, too. He painted very much the same way as Mommy—with the brush in someone else's hand.

Conclusion:
If at first you don't succeed, get someone else to do it.

The Man in Our Dumpster

When I was growing up, Daddy, Mommy, and all of us kids (sometimes we were four, sometimes we were six or seven) lived in a big house with 13 rooms in Salinas, California. When we finished growing up, Daddy got a hankering for the forest and Mommy got a hankering to give up cleaning 13 rooms all the time. So, they decided to buy an RV, travel when they could, and park it in the woods of Arroyo Seco at other times.

Moving out of 13 rooms was big business. Daddy and Mommy had quite a list of things to do: cleaning, giving away or selling stuff that would not fit in the RV, packing things to take with them, throwing away trash, and lots of other things (like changing addresses with businesses and the post office). One day when Daddy was out doing the lots of other things, Mommy held a yard sale. One of the people who came to the yard sale buys things to send to a community in the Philippines. He buys lots of things to send there because there are lots of people who need help. He made a deal with Mommy to come back and pick up whatever did not get sold.

He was as good as his word. Half an hour after the sale ended, he came with a big truck and took most of the remaining big items, which Mommy sold to him real cheap or gave to him. Then, he drove the truck home and walked back. He had remembered seeing a huge dumpster in our yard. Daddy had ordered the dumpster so that we could throw out the things that were not good anymore. The dumpster was almost full. Our neighbor asked Mommy if he could have the things in the dumpster that he might be able to fix, and Mommy said okay.

When Daddy came home, boy, was he surprised to see a man he did not know, standing in our dumpster, and holding things up from time to time, calling out to Mommy, "Bettee, why you t'row deez away?"

Conclusion:
Dumpsters make good neighbors.

MOMMY'S CLOTHING CALAMITIES

Shenan (CB) Leaver (with Betty Lou Leaver)

A Personalized View
of San Francisco

When visitors come from out of town, Mommy likes to show them around San Francisco. She says a personal tour with a friend who knows and likes the city makes a visit to San Francisco very personalized and more interesting.

One of the exciting things Mommy does with our guests is to ride the cable cars. These are unique to San Francisco. If you don't live in San Francisco, maybe you have seen the cable cars on "Three's Company."

Very early in her experience as tour guide for visiting friends, a cable car ride taught her how to dress for San Francisco. What happened was that Mommy and her friend hopped onto one of the Hyde Street cable cars as it headed down the long hill toward Fisherman's Wharf. There was no room on the benches in the cable car for either of them to sit, so they had to stand and hang onto the poles that are near the edges of each car. Mommy's friend grabbed one pole, and Mommy grabbed another. They rode down the hill, standing on the side of the cable car, and holding on to the poles.

Suddenly, one of those mischievous breezes that run around San Francisco at all hours grabbed Mommy's long summer dress and pulled it up over her head. Mommy could not fight the breeze because she had to hang onto the pole with one hand and onto her purse and bags with the other. So, Mommy rode all the way to Fisherman's Wharf with her dress up, not down.

Mommy's friend said the cable car ride gave him a good view of San Francisco, as well as a good view in San Francisco. Mommy now wears pants or shorts when she takes visitors to San Francisco.

Conclusion:
A gentle little breeze can be very strong!

In a Hurry

Mommy says that we kept her very busy, the four of us, when we were little, and that whenever she got things accomplished on time, she felt it was an achievement. When she got things done early, she knew it had to be a miracle — or a significant missing detail. Usually, it was the latter.

One morning she was very pleased with herself. For some reason, she was very efficient. We were all awake, washed, dressed, fed, and standing in line for our various school buses with our lunch boxes in hand, and Mommy had more time than usual before she had to leave for her bus stop.

While our buses were picking us up, she quickly dressed. Mommy always dresses quickly. When the last bus departed, she had ten extra minutes to make her bus, so she strolled to the bus stop. (She usually ran up to the bus just in time to pop into it before the door closed.)

When she got to the bus stop, she sat down on the bench very ladylike, as if she did this every day instead of rushing up out of breath and disheveled. The bus stop was located on a Lee Highway, a major thoroughfare through Arlington, Virginia, where we lived at that time, so there were always lots of people around. Some of them Mommy recognized because they rode the bus often.

This morning one of the women she sometimes talked to asked if she had not forgotten something. Mommy wondered what it was that she usually brought that she did not have with her that day. She checked. She had her purse, her briefcase, even her spare umbrella, since it rained often in Washington in the fall.

"Well," she said to the lady, "I cannot imagine what it might be. I seem to have everything I usually have."

"I don't think so," said the lady and asked, "What about your skirt?"

Mommy ran home, really fast. This time, she was out of breath going away from the bus stop, not coming up to it.

Conclusion:
Credit cards are not the only things that one should not leave home without.

Escape from a Hungry Escalator

Once Mommy went to Brasilia in Brazil to do some teaching. She really liked being in Brasilia. It was summer, so she spent her spare time walking, sightseeing, and shopping. It was the shopping part that got Mommy into trouble one day. She wore a long black skirt. (At least, that day Mommy remembered not to leave home without her skirt). The skirt was pretty for teaching, and it was okay for shopping. It would probably have been okay for elevators.

The shopping mall, however, did not have elevators. It had escalators. After doing some shopping on the top floor, Mommy got on one of the escalators to go down to another floor to do some more shopping.

As Mommy rode down the escalator, she was talking to a friend who had come to the shopping mall with her. They must have been talking about something very interesting because Mommy did not notice what was happening with her skirt.

What was happening? Well, one of the mean stairs on the escalator reached up and grabbed the bottom of her skirt. Of course, it was really long, and Mommy is really short. So, she did not notice that at first.

As the escalator moved along slowly, the stair slowly chewed away at the bottom of the skirt. Slowly it pulled more in. Slowly Mommy's skirt slipped away from her waist.

By the time Mommy reached the end of the escalator, she was wearing a layered look: light blue blouse from neck to waist, white slip from waist to knee, and black skirt from knee to escalator stair. That's when she noticed that her skirt was slowly slipping away into the jaws of the escalator.

That scared Mommy. (I think she also did not like the layered look.) She grabbed her skirt with both hands and yanked it out of the jaws of the escalator. The escalator threw up the stair that was gobbling Mommy's skirt.

Then, the whole escalator stopped moving. People started walking down the stairs. Mommy, too, but she had only one more stair to go to reach the bottom.

That is the story of how Mommy managed to give some shoppers extra exercise on one summer day in Brasilia. Mommy said that when people started walking down the stairs, she was a little embarrassed. I asked Mommy what she did at that point. She said that she kept on walking, pretending that she had nothing at all to do with what happened to the elevator.

Hmm... I think that must run in the family because I heard a story like that about Great Grandma Germon once. Someone told me—I think it was Grandma—that Great Grandma Germon lived in the days when ladies' underpants were held together by pins. Well, one day one of those pins broke when she was walking out of the theater, and her underpants fell right onto the sidewalk. Great Grandma calmly stepped over them, as if they had been lying there all along, and, like Mommy, just kept on walking.

Conclusion:
If you hold your head high and don't look down, maybe no one will notice what you don't want them to see.

In Plain View

Mommy really does have trouble with details. This is especially true if she cannot see them.

One time Mommy was invited to a posh hotel to deliver a speech in Washington, D.C. Mommy dressed up very fancy. She looked very nice. She gave her speech, and she left the posh hotel. For some reason, maybe because the weather was very nice, she decided to walk the mile to the metro station.

First, though, Mommy stopped off at the bathroom. There, she combed her hair, washed her hands, and put her backpack on. (Mommy almost always carries a backpack.) Then, she left the posh hotel.

As Mommy walked through the hotel lobby, people smiled. Mommy thought that they were being friendly. Well, maybe she did look a little funny in fancy clothes, high heel shoes, and a backpack. That did not bother Mommy. She was used to people thinking that she looked funny carrying a backpack when she was all dressed up.

Mommy walked all the way down Massachusetts Avenue to the metro station. People smiled at her on the way, and she smiled and waved back. It was such a nice day, and she was having such a nice walk. Why would she not want to smile?

When she got to the metro station, some nice lady came up to her and told her that she was having problems with her skirt again. She told Mommy that the back of her skirt and slip were rolled up behind her backpack. Mommy did not check that detail before leaving the bathroom; after all, she could not see the skirt in the back. And that is how Mommy ended up prancing about the nation's capital in her pink panties.

Conclusion:
Watching where you are going is not always enough.
Sometimes you also have to check your back side!

Casual Attire

Mommy gets invited to parties a lot. Sometimes she has to dress up real fancy. Other times, the invitation says "casual attire."

One time when Mommy got a casual attire invitation for a party with some business associates, she was staying with my sister. She did not have any casual clothes with her—just things that were for play and fun. It seems to me that play clothes are "casual," but Mommy said no. She wanted something a little dressier in order to be casual.

So, Mommy went shopping. There were some nice stores where my sister was living. Sometimes it is hard for Mommy to find just exactly what she wants, but this time was different. She found a very pretty pink pantsuit. The pantsuit fit her perfectly. It did not cost a lot, either.

The next night, it was time for the party. Mommy put on her pretty pink pantsuit. Mommy said it was very comfortable—that was another reason she really liked it. She thinks it is very difficult to find good-looking clothes that are also comfortable.

My sister was not home, but that did not matter. Mommy got a ride to the party.

Mommy had a good time at the party. There were people there she did not know, but she expected that. The purpose of the party was to introduce her to new business associates in the area she was visiting. All the guests were very friendly, and all of them smiled at her. When Mommy did not know someone who smiled at her, she went over and introduced herself. Mommy likes to talk to people who smile at her.

Mommy had a very good time. She met some friendly new people. The food was good. The conversation was interesting. The party lasted several hours, and Mommy stayed until the very end, getting to meet a number of new business associates. She said she hoped she had made an impression on them.

When Mommy came back, my sister was already home and in bed. She got up when she heard Mommy come in. When she saw Mommy, she was very surprised.

"Where were you?" she asked.

"At a business reception," said Mommy.

"In that outfit?"

"Sure," said Mommy. "It is really very comfortable. Feel how soft it is."

"Mom!" said my sister. "Of course, it is comfortable and soft. It's pajamas!"

Conclusion:
If the clothes are really soft, they must be pajamas.

That Doggone Skirt

Mommy really does have trouble with her skirts. It does not matter whether she is in Washington, DC, Brazil, or any other city in the world.

I can give you an example. It is a very simple story. It is the kind of thing that could happen to any one, just the way it happened to Mommy—except the ending of the story is always different with Mommy for some reason.

Here is the example that I promised. It was a very uneventful day (well, uneventful for Mommy) in Bloomington, Indiana, where Mommy was doing some consulting for Indiana University. Mommy doesn't like the weather there a whole lot, but she goes there, anyway.

This day, though, the weather was very nice, and Mommy decided to have lunch away from her office. She walked to one of the restaurants in town. As she walked through town, she saw a lot of people on the street. Everyone liked the nice weather.

Some of the people were walking their dogs. One very nice German shepherd dog was trotting very nicely down the street beside his owners when he saw Mommy. He came over to talk to her. She likes German shepherds, so she talked to him. He jumped up on her, and she petted him. Then they parted company.

Mommy went on to the restaurant. A lot of people were in the restaurant. They were very happy on this nice day. They all smiled at Mommy, and Mommy said "hi" to them. Then she had her lunch and went back to her office.

Shenan (CB) Leaver (with Betty Lou Leaver)

On the way back to her office, lots more people smiled at her. She was just beginning to think how nice it was to see so many happy people when she reached the office. One of her colleagues looked at her skirt and asked her, "Do you realize that your skirt is torn open in the back?"

Not again! Mommy forgot to check her backside again—and I told her after her pink-panty experience in Washington that she should always, always check her backside.

Conclusion:
If you don't learn your lesson the first time, you may get another chance to learn it—but you may not like the circumstances.

MOMMY'S MISSING DETAILS

CB—

We need a graphic
for this page!

Mom

Shenan (CB) Leaver (with Betty Lou Leaver)

Raindrops Keep Falling on Her Head

Once upon a time Mommy worked at NASA in Houston, Texas for a year. She liked her work, but she did not like the Houston climate. It rained a lot. In fact, it rained off and on nearly every day in the spring.

Being from California, Mommy was not used to that much rain. She figured out how to cope, however. She bought a small umbrella that folded up to fit inside her backpack. That way, if it rained, she could quickly pull out the umbrella, and if it did not rain, the umbrella would be out of the way in her backpack. This was especially helpful because Mommy walked back and forth from work. She liked walking, but she often got caught in surprise rainstorms.

One day it was not raining when Mommy left her house. In fact, it was pretty hot.

Mommy had a long walk. She lived more than two miles from NASA. When she walked, she thought a lot. She thought about work, about her family, about lots of things. So, she did not pay a lot of attention to what was going on around her. (That is probably why a lot of detail-oblivious people get called absent-minded.)

Mommy got pretty used to doing things automatically, without thinking, while she walked, so that she could think about the things that she wanted to. When the cars stopped moving, she sensed a red light and crossed the street, and when her skin felt wet, she sensed the rain and put up her umbrella. It all worked out pretty well.

On this day that I am talking about, though, she was already at NASA, and there had been no rain. Somewhere in her subconscious, she was thinking about how great it was to have a morning without rain. Then, suddenly her skin felt wet, and her automatic reaction took over. Out came the umbrella and on Mommy walked.

Mommy felt pretty good about her quick reaction to the sudden rain, until she noticed that people had stopped walking around the buildings and were looking at her strangely. That was when she realized that she was walking through a sprinkler with her umbrella up.

Conclusion:
Make sure it is raining before you put up your umbrella.

The Babysitter

When I was smaller, Mommy sent me to church every Sunday morning. The church van always came at 9:15 to pick me up, and Mommy was always rushing to get me ready on time.

One Sunday morning a man came to the door at 9:10. Mommy could not believe that the van was five minutes early. She always counted on those five minutes to get me ready. Usually, no one came to the door, so she figured that they must have been sitting there for a while. She started to hurry.

"Just a minute," she said, leaving the door open. She quickly grabbed my suit coat and put it on me.

"I just have to comb his hair; it will just be a second," she called to the man at the door as she darted into the bathroom after a comb. A few seconds later, I looked mighty spiffy.

"Almost ready," she called out again, as she rushed upstairs to get my Bible and offering.

Whew! She had never got me ready so fast.

"Here he is," she said, out of breath, as she pushed me out the door.

I looked up at a tall man in blue. I did not know him, so I just stood and looked at him, and he looked at Mommy.

"Ma'am," he said, now that he could get a word in edgewise. "All I require is a signature." He was an express mail postman with a package for Mommy.

A friend of Mommy says that every time she sees an express mail truck now she thinks that there goes Mommy's babysitter. She also said that Mommy was not going to get Mother of the Year Award that year.

Conclusion:
Not everyone can be Mother of the Year!

Things That Grow

When my sister was in kindergarten, she invited a new friend to stay overnight. They played a lot. Then, they got bored.

My mommy wanted them to have a good time, so she promised to take them to see a movie. My sister and her friend were very excited!

Mommy made the promise before she knew whether there were any children's movies playing in town, so she had to look in all the newspapers. She looked and looked. She could not find any children's movies playing.

Finally, Mommy found a good movie at a movie theatre she had never been to before. She was so pleased! The movie was about Pinocchio. She knew we all liked the story of Pinocchio. So, all of us got dressed up pretty—even Daddy!

We got into the car. Mommy had directions and told Daddy where to go. None of us had ever been in that part of town before, so it took a little time and effort to find the theatre. It was an outdoors theatre and sort of hidden away from view.

When we arrived, the movie was about to start. My sister and her friend became even more excited.

We drove up to the marquee. When we saw it, we became very excited. Big, red letters told us we had found the Pinocchio film. Mommy read the red letters and changed her mind about taking us to see the movie. She told Daddy to turn around and drive away, and he did so immediately.

Mommy and Daddy took us to Baskin-Robbins instead of

the movie. I like ice cream very much, so that was okay with me. My sister and her friend, though, would have preferred the movie. They did not understand why Mommy changed her mind, and Mommy could not explain it very well. She said that some day they would understand why the words on the marquee had made her change her mind.

The marquee said, "Pinocchio: It wasn't his nose that grew!" So, what grew?

Conclusion:
Sometimes you just cannot figure out parents.

A Missing Pigtail

When my mommy was in kindergarten, she often got into a lot of trouble without even trying to do that. Lots of aunts and uncles have told me the story of Mommy and the trouble she always got into. They all remembered especially gleefully the incident of the missing pigtail.

It seems that my mommy liked to play games. She played all kinds of games, and almost all of them got her in trouble.

Once she played seamstress. She got into trouble that time because she told one of the boys in the neighborhood that she was making doll dresses and selling them for a quarter. That boy liked her, so he got a quarter from his mother and rang Mommy's doorbell.

"Hello," he told Grandma and held out his hand with a quarter in it, asking to see some of Mommy's best dresses. Boy, was Grandma confused!

Another time Mommy played homemaker. That time she got into trouble by accidentally running my aunt's arm through the wringer of the wringer-washing machine. Fortunately, the wringer broke, so my aunt's arm did not.

One day Mommy decided to play beauty shop. She talked my aunt into playing with her. Yes, it was the same aunt she talked into putting her arm into the wringer. (Yes, that aunt did live to grow up, in spite of my mommy's games.) My mommy styled my aunt's hair in lots of different ways. Then she thought my aunt might look better in short hair, so she took a pair of scissors and cut off one pigtail. That did not look better, so she left the other pigtail. While Mommy was trying to figure out how to get the cut-off pigtail reattached, Grandma called for my aunt to come and help her do something.

"What are we going to do about the pigtail?" my aunt asked, worried.

"Oh, don't worry," Mommy told her. "Ma is too stupid to notice a missing pigtail."

My aunt went off to help my Grandmother. She helped her for a couple hours. Grandma kept looking at her but said nothing. She thought something about my aunt looked different. Finally, she figured it out.

"What happened to your pigtail?" she asked, very upset.

My aunt started crying. She explained that Grandma was not supposed to notice. She said that my mommy had promised that Grandma would not notice because she was too dumb to notice. However, Grandma did notice, and Mommy got into a lot of trouble—again. Mommy said that she did not know whether she got into more trouble for cutting off the pigtail or for saying that Grandma would be too dumb to notice.

I guess Mommy did not know then that it is not Grandma who misses details. It is Mommy who misses them.

Conclusion:
It is not a good idea to think that your mother is dumb
and a worse idea to say that she is.

The Empty Chair

One of the details that Mommy used to miss a lot was supper. We hated it when Mommy tried to put us to bed and had forgotten to feed us supper. We always reminded her, and she always made it for us. We wanted her to remember, though, without us telling her, just like we wanted her to remember to put filling in our sandwiches—sometimes she would send us to school, having forgotten the filling in one or another sandwich. My sister used to call these special, forgetful concoctions of Mommy's "air sandwiches."

One time she did remember to make supper. She made a very nice supper for us. We were so happy.

We were all seated around the table, but there was an empty chair. It belonged to Daddy. He was not home from work yet.

Mommy looked at her watch. She thought it was very strange that he was not home yet, since it was already 9:00 at night. He usually got off work at 5:00 and was home shortly after that.

"Well, let's go ahead and eat," Mommy said. "Your father will show up some time. He must be working late, or maybe he ran into some bad traffic. He is working in a new place, and it is at least half an hour from here."

Mommy could not call Daddy, and Daddy could not call Mommy. We had just moved into a new house, and we would not have a phone for a couple more days while we were waiting for the phone company to install it. So, all Mommy could do was wait for Daddy to show up. She sat down to eat with us.

We were all in the middle of eating our dinner quietly, when Mommy jumped up. She seemed very agitated.

"Oh, my goodness! Oh, my goodness!" she repeated several times. "I know why he isn't here! I was supposed to pick him up!"

Mommy ran out the door. We all wondered how mad Daddy would be when Mommy arrived. He wasn't mad, though. He was very sad. He thought he was going to have to spend the night on the bench outside his office. Boy, was he happy to see Mommy! (Well, and maybe a little bit mad, too.)

Conclusion:
Empty chairs mean that something (or someone) is missing.

Faulty Impressions

Once Mommy was responsible for a group of Senators' wives who were visiting the Soviet Union. Mommy was supposed to make sure that everything went just perfect for them. However, that is a very difficult thing to do when you are Mommy because anything that can go wrong will go wrong and even what is perfectly normal will somehow get turned upside down to become abnormal.

The trip with the senators' wives was no different from Mommy's personal travel experiences. There were the missing details and the unexplained and unusual happenings. I remember three things that Mommy told me about the trip. Three "events" make a lot of sense. After all, Mommy went to three different cities—and one "event" per city is pretty low on the Mommy Geiger counter.

The first event that helped toward Mommy making an "impression" on the group of ladies happened in Moscow. These ladies were very interested in everything, but they were pretty nervous about being alone because they did not speak Russian. They depended on Mommy for that. That worked okay because they went everywhere in a group. Well, almost everywhere. Once they were taking a metro from one part of the city to another. The Moscow metros tend to get very full, and the doors sometimes close awfully fast. Probably that is why the trains can come all the time just two minutes apart. (Mommy says that no other place she has been has as good a metro system as Moscow in that respect.) Well, the ladies did not have to wait very long before a train showed up—just seconds within their arrival on the platform. Mommy looked around and counted. Yes, all 15 ladies were there. The doors opened, and Mommy pushed everyone on. They were too many! Everyone was in except Mommy and one lady. That lady did not fit. Well, she could have fit if she had crushed herself in the way Musvovites do. So, Mommy got in, pulling the lady along with her. Then, the oh-oh happened. The doors started to close, and the lady panicked, letting go of Mommy's hand. When the doors were all closed, Mommy and everyone else were on the inside, looking out at the forlorn lady on the platform. Poor Mommy! She kept her face pressed to the door all the way to the next station, then had everyone wait while she went back to scoop up the timid lady—but the lady was gone! Boy, was Mommy worried—until they all get back to the hotel, and the lady was waiting for them. She had shown a cab driver the matchbook from the hotel, and he took her there. Whew! Mommy did not want to have to explain to *anyone* how or why she lost a senator's wife in Moscow.

Next, Mommy had a second chance to make an impression on these ladies. They all went to Leningrad (now called St. Petersburg, like it was in the pre-Soviet days) to tour the city. There was a tour guide who spoke English but not very well, and Mommy had to help her a lot. In Leningrad, the ladies happened to meet a little old lady and wanted Mommy to talk to her. She did, and she found out that the little old lady had survived the World War II blockade of Leningrad by Hitler's troops. The ladies wanted to hear all about that. So did the camera crew from an American television station that had come along with them. So, Mommy agreed to be an interpreter (although she does not like to interpret because she misses little details—well, you know that already). The little old lady talked and talked, the camera rolled and rolled, and Mommy looked at the camera and the ladies and interpreted the little old lady's words in English. Only, everyone stared at her, not understanding. It seems that Mommy did not translate the words but explained in simple Russian, like she was talking to students, what the old lady had said in more complex Russian. The camera kept rolling, and Mommy was very embarrassed when she realized what she was doing. One little mistake — and an impression one makes!

Then, if there were any doubts left about my mommy, they all disappeared when she took the ladies to Tashkent, Uzbekistan, which, at that time, was part of the Soviet Union. One night, the ladies were tired from all the sightseeing and meetings (in both Tashkent and Moscow, they had set up meetings with city officials), and decided that they would like to do something very American, like seeing a movie (although it is not clear how they would have been able to understand it). Mommy began to redeem herself immediately. She found a movie theater right away, and she found a slapstick comedy (the ladies just might be able to understand a lot of that). They were late. Everyone else was already inside watching the movie — and laughing a lot. Mommy bought the ladies' tickets, and then they went inside. There was no ticket collector there! The entrance was empty! Mommy found a door and opened it. There we were stairs leading up to a platform; Mommy figured that was the way in and walked up the stairs and across the platform with a queue of ladies in town. She could not see the movie screen yet and nothing was in front of her except more platform, but she kept walking, and the ladies kept following. Then she realized that people were laughing a lot louder than before, and she looked left, toward the laughter. There was the audience, and there, in the middle of the platform, were some stairs leading down to seats! She led her queue across the platform and down the stairs, and the audience laughed and clapped. When she got to some empty seats where they could sit, she sat down and found herself facing the screen, in front of which was her queue, person by person walking across the stage in front of the screen like a gaggle of goslings, their shadows showing up as if they were part of the movie. It was a good-natured crowd, and when everyone had sat down, the audience laughed some more and clapped for them. Now, there was Mommy's final impression.

Oh, well, at least, people did not forget that trip. Isn't that what is important about traveling—remembering what you saw and did?

Conclusion:
Pay attention to details and you will make an impression;
miss details and you will make a memory.

ON THE ROAD
WITH MOMMY

Shenan (CB) Leaver (with Betty Lou Leaver)

Those Darn Keys

I do not know how to drive, but I do know that there are three rules that are important for driving. First, you have to have the keys, or you cannot drive at all. Second, you have to get the car started, or you do not go anywhere at all. Third, you have to know where you are going or have a map, or you do not get to the right place. I think Mommy knows these rules, too, but it seems like she forgets a lot.

With keys (rule #1), for example, she locks them inside the car so often that Daddy bought her a little box with a spare key to hide somewhere on the car. She also has locked me in the car by accident and had to call the police to get me out. She has locked my sister in the car by accident and called the police to get her out. (The police have come to know Mommy pretty well, and they just shake their heads when they come and see who it is.) She has locked my brother in the car, too, but he figured out how to get out all by himself.

The little black box works, though, but sometimes Mommy drives a different car without a little box. Then she is in trouble again.

Once Mommy returned to a non-little-black-box car from the bookstore, only to find the car locked. She looked in her purse for the keys, but they were not there. Then she saw keys inside on the seat. Oh, oh! It was Sunday, and it would be hard to find someone to help. The car was lock-safe, so she could not pick the lock. So, Mommy looked in the telephone book and found a locksmith who would come help her if she would pay him a lot of money.

She agreed. He came and unlocked the door, although he broke the lock, so then, Mommy had to get the lock fixed. Mommy thanked him and paid him, anyway. She was just glad to get the keys so that she could drive home.

With relief, she picked the keys up from the seat—but they were the wrong keys. With a sigh, Mommy went back to the bookstore.

It was now almost two hours after she had left the store, and if her keys were in the store, she could have saved two hours of time. As it turned out, she could have saved those two hours because the information desk had the keys. They asked Mommy what she would do to get them back, and she said, "Just about anything." They made Mommy jump up and down and bark like a dog to get her keys back. I bet a lot of shoppers thought she was crazy. Maybe they were right!

Conclusion:
It is better to have the keys outside the car than in it
unless you are already in it, too.

The Car That Would Not Start

Rule for the road #2 says that in order to get somewhere, you have to be able to start the car. That means, of course, that you already have the keys. Sometimes that is difficult for Mommy to keep both of these rules straight.

Once she returned to the parking lot after work to find that she did not have the keys to the car. Before going back to the office, she looked inside. Sure enough, there were the keys. At least with this car, she knew how to break in and get the keys. In a little while, she was inside, but the car would not start (rule #2). It was now pretty late, and there were not very many people around. Mommy went to the garage attendant and asked if he knew someone who could give her a jump.

"Are you driving that brown van on the top level?" he asked.

"Yeah!" Mommy was surprised that he knew which car she drove.

"Well, you're out of gas," he said.

"How's that?" she asked. How could he know she was out of gas? Besides, the car had not been on empty when she parked it.

He did know. He explained, "Because you left the keys in the ignition with the car running and the door locked. We tried to get in but could not. The car finally ran out of gas in the middle of the afternoon."

Oops! He probably thought that Mommy was crazy. Maybe he was right.

Conclusion:
When you are at work, it is better to have your keys in your pocket than in your car.

Maps in the Head

When Mommy remembers the keys and does get the car started, she often goes to new places. That's where rule #3 comes in: know where you are going.

One day she took a new colleague, Peter, from her office in Washington, D.C. to Annapolis, Maryland for a meeting. They had a very good meeting. Both had to be home for other meetings in the early evening, however, so they left in the late afternoon. That was good timing. They could miss rush-hour traffic (although there is not much rush-hour traffic in Annapolis) and be back in Washington, D.C. in plenty of time.

They drove out to Route 50 and headed for home. Mommy drove and drove. Washington should be showing up pretty soon. Sure enough, buildings came into sight.

"Look," Mommy said. "We're almost there."

"But those don't look like any Washington buildings I've seen," Peter said. Of course, he was new to Washington, so he did not really know what all the buildings in Washington looked like.

"I don't recognize them, either," said Mommy. "But we're coming in from a different direction than I am used to."

They drove further, and the buildings got nearer. None of those other buildings looked familiar, either. Suddenly, there was water—and ocean—in front of the car.

"Hey, wait a minute! Washington isn't on the ocean!" said Peter.

"But it's not that far from the ocean," said Mommy.

Pretty soon a sign appeared. Peter said, "I think we're in Baltimore."

He was right. The sign said, "Welcome to Baltimore."

"One little mistake..." answered Mommy. (That one little mistake meant that they got home really late and missed their meetings.)

Mommy also sometimes goes long distances. Once she and a colleague, Ellen, drove from Pittsburgh to a conference at Northwestern University north of Chicago. Mommy sort of knew the road in general, so they took off and drove for a couple of hours. Somewhere inside the state of Ohio, Mommy asked Ellen to look at the map.

"Where is the map?" asked Ellen.

"I thought you were bringing a map," Mommy said.

"No, I thought you were bringing the map," Ellen replied.

Oops! Well, they did make it without a map and without mishap all the way to the exact building where the conference was being held.

Mommy was quite pleased. She was also pretty certain that she would find the road back just fine. She should not have been.

As they were driving along, Ellen said, "I think we're in Michigan." (Michigan was not one of the states that they were supposed to be going through.)

"That cannot be," said Mommy.

"So, why does the highway sign say Michigan Route 94?" asked Ellen.

"Because that exit goes to Route 94," answered Mommy.

They drove a little further. Then Ellen had another question.

"The exit there says Gerald Ford Expressway," she noted. "Wasn't Gerald Ford from Michigan?"

"The exit must go to the Gerald Ford Expressway," Mommy explained patiently.

They drove still further. Soon there was a big highway sign with mileage to Battle Creek, Kalamazoo, and Detroit. Mommy admitted that they were probably in Michigan. Ellen probably thought that Mommy was crazy. She may have been right.

Conclusion:
Maps in the car are better than maps in the head!

Shenan (CB) Leaver (with Betty Lou Leaver)

The Power of Observation

Once my sister, Echo, had learned to drive, she was much more observant than my mommy was. She belongs to that group of people that Mommy calls detail-observant, so she pays very close attention to all kinds of things that Mommy does not notice at all.

One night after work, my mommy and Echo were driving home together. Well, Mommy, the *grande dame* of detail-obliviousness, was doing the driving, and clearly, it was Echo, the detail-observant, who was doing the watching. That is pretty typical of how they usually drive together.

At the light where Mommy had to make a turn to get onto the highway coming to our town—she and Echo worked in the next town over—there was a long line of cars. That was no surprise. There often was a long line at this particular light, especially right after work, so Mommy was sort of expecting a line, anyway.

Mommy could see all the way to the intersection, and the light there was red. So, she got into line behind the cars. She waited and waited.

The light turned green, but the cars in front of her did not move.

After work, Mommy is sometimes patient. So, she waited through another change of lights, while talking to my sister.

Again, the line did not move. Mommy continued to talk to Echo and just waited.

"What are you doing?" Echo asked her.

"I am waiting for the line to move," Mommy explained.

"But, Mom," Echo said, looking out her window and figuring out what was going on, "all these cars are parked. You're sitting at the end of a row of parking spaces along the street."

Oops! Those little details fool Mommy every time!

Conclusion:
If you want to make it home, don't line up behind a row of parked cars.

The Value of an Open Ear on the Open Road

Mommy talks a lot, including in a lot of different languages, but she does not listen very well. At least, that's what Daddy says. He is probably right. After all, he has some very good examples of when Mommy did not listen when she should have.

Many years ago Mommy and Daddy were returning to Montana, where they were living at the time, from visiting my grandparents in Maine. Daddy usually does not like to let Mommy drive, especially if he is asleep. You can probably figure out why.

Mommy and Daddy drove through many northern states. It was winter, and driving was tough. Daddy did all right, but Mommy sometimes had problems when it was her turn. For example, she fishtailed across the entire state of Iowa. Daddy kept telling her to pull over and let him drive, but she could not get stopped until she reached South Dakota. Then she did.

When Daddy got to Wyoming, he was really tired. He had driven most of the way, except for the sled ride across the state of Iowa, and he could not sleep in Iowa because he did not like Mommy's crooked steering. It made him nervous.

In Wyoming, however, he got really, really sleepy, so he decided he could let Mommy drive again. That was a mistake.

As soon as Mommy started to drive, it started to snow. It snowed and snowed.

As soon as Mommy started to drive, Daddy started to sleep. He slept and slept.

So, Mommy drove while it snowed and Daddy slept. Pretty soon, she was driving high in the mountains. There was snow everywhere and no place to stop. She turned on the radio. The radio said that Wyoming was getting the biggest snowstorm in 100 years.

Daddy woke up for a minute, and Mommy told him that it was snowing too much to drive. He told her to pull off in a rest area, and then he went back to sleep.

Mommy found a sign that said rest area. She pulled over, but it was not an on-road rest area. It was an exit. She drove off the exit and down another road, where she saw a rest area. It was full of snow, and she could not get in.

Mommy wanted to turn around and get back on the highway, but she did not know whether the road she was on was one-way or two-way. She could not stop to look at the map because the road was isolated. If she stopped and got stuck, they would not be able to get any help.

After another 4-5 miles, driven very slowly, Daddy woke up. He asked Mommy where they were. She said that she did not know. He looked ahead. There was nothing but a road leading into the wilderness with no tracks at all in the snow. He looked behind. There was only a road through the wilderness with only our tracks.

Daddy was not happy. He said that he told Mommy to stop at a rest area, not get off the road. Mommy did not think that there was a big difference, but Daddy did.

Daddy figured out that we were on a two-way road. We turned around and went back to the highway, and Daddy took over the driving.

Daddy no longer sleeps when Mommy drives. He especially does not sleep when Mommy is driving in snow.

All the same, Daddy has continued to drive with Mommy. I have to tell you, though, that he has also continued to be frustrated that Mommy still does not listen to him very well when she is driving.

One time, several years after the Wyoming experience, Daddy changed places with Mommy at a gas station in Nevada. He did not plan to sleep, but he did want to rest. However, they were driving a very small truck at that time, and the only place to rest was the covered truck bed. Daddy crawled into the back, as Mommy pulled out of the gas station.

As Mommy blinked to turn back onto the highway, Daddy began pounding on the window. Mommy figured she would stop and see what he wanted as soon as she was back on the highway and could pull over, but he stopped pounding once she merged. Then, she found out why he had been pounding: She had got on the highway going in the wrong direction—back where they had come from. Worse, the next exit was ten miles away!

Daddy no longer rests when Mommy is driving. He especially does not rest when he cannot sit right beside Mommy.

Conclusion:
Sometimes it is wise to listen, even when you think you already know something.

Shenan (CB) Leaver (with Betty Lou Leaver)

The Three-Event Trip

Now it has become my brother's turn to drive with Mommy. Last summer he and Mommy drove to see my sister in Illinois. As always with Mommy, it was an eventful trip. In fact, it was a three-event trip.

Daddy and Mommy had just acquired a 20-year-old truck, a "dually." Daddy told Mommy not to take it to Illinois, but Mommy drove it and thought it was working just fine. Besides, my sister needed to have some things brought to her that she had left in storage when she moved from San Diego to Illinois. Mommy planned a weeklong trip, which is how much time my brother could take off from work.

Off Mommy and my brother went one Saturday morning in August. They swooped through San Diego, picking up my sister's belongings there. Then they headed out through the Mojave Desert in the middle of the hottest month of the year in a truck without air conditioning. My brother was beginning to agree with Daddy about Mommy and traveling. It was so hot that both their eyeballs dried out, making seeing to drive difficult. It was not easy to breathe, either.

Finally, they made it out of the desert. They crossed into Arizona, where they passed a lot of state prisons. At the exit to each state prison was a sign, "Do not pick up hitchhikers." My brother thinks that the state prisons in Arizona must have a security problem.

After Arizona, they began driving across a big Indian reservation in New Mexico. They were beginning to enjoy the drive very much, when steam started pouring out of the hood. The truck stopped, and there they were—miles from nowhere. Daddy was going to tell Mommy, "I told you so."

A long tow and two days later, as well as several hundred dollars lighter, they set out once again for Illinois—and they made it. Mommy was relieved. The truck was working. She could answer Daddy, "Well, we only had one little problem."

After giving my sister her stuff and staying overnight, Mommy and my brother left for California. They drove mile after mile through the cornfields of Illinois. Then they reached the cornfields of Iowa, where, miles from nowhere, the lights on the truck went out and would not come back on. Daddy was definitely going to tell Mommy, "I told you so."

A long tow and a half-day later, as well as a couple of hundred dollars lighter, they set out once again for California. Would they make it? My brother analyzed the situation. They were breaking down exactly every 1400 miles. He checked the next 1400-mile point: Skull Valley, Utah. He did not like that name. He said that no way did he want to break down in Skull Valley.

Sure enough, when Mommy and my brother reached the Utah border, the truck started to sputter. My brother said it was the carburetor, and that he was *not*, repeat *not*, going to be stuck in a place called Skull Valley. He got out and tinkered with the carburetor.

They made it through Skull Valley and over the California mountains. The truck kept chugging along until it reached Lodi, California, where it lay down on the job and refused to move any more. It would need extensive repairs, so Daddy went to pick up Mommy and my brother.

What could Daddy say? He told Mommy so?

Conclusion:
Sometimes Father knows best.

The Driver

So, who said Mommy does not drive well? Definitely Daddy. Perhaps also the guy who tested her for her first license in Montana, although he did give her a license. I think he was just happy that she took the time to come in and get a license. A lot of folks in that part of Montana back then simply drove; they did not worry about getting a license. The greatest number of reported "crimes" in that area was people caught driving without a license.

So, Mommy was a good citizen. She went in to get her license. She passed the written test with 100%. That's Mommy. She does well on written tests. Performance tests, though, can have different results.

The tester took Mommy out for a test drive around the courthouse. The first thing Mommy did was to drive through a stop sign. (I guess it was another one of those details that Mommy misses.) The tester was nice, though. He said that since there was a truck parked right near the stop sign, perhaps it had blocked her vision. Mommy did not say anything. The stop sign was the one right in front of her house, so she did know it was there. She just forgot about it. (Besides, when she was on foot, she walked whenever she saw a stop sign.)

The next thing the tester wanted was for Mommy to parallel park the car. He had her drive up to a space between two police cars. Daddy had taught Mommy how to parallel park, but she had never been able to do it. This time, though, she was very afraid that she would hit one of the parked police cars, so she was very careful and parallel parked the car perfectly. The tester was quite surprised and impressed. So was Mommy.

Then he had Mommy drive back to the courthouse so he could prepare her license. As they came up to the courthouse, Mommy looked to where the tester was pointing. He wanted her to angle park. Daddy had not shown Mommy how to do that, but it did not look too difficult. So, Mommy took aim and pulled in. She did pretty well; she fit the car in the lines. However, she did not fit it equidistant between the cars on either side of her. She had lots of room on her side to get out, but the tester had none on his side. He had to crawl out Mommy's side of the car. Still, he gave her a license.

Mommy did not know how to back out of the angle parking space, so she walked home. Daddy walked over after work and drove the car home. Some time later, Mommy learned how to drive.

Conclusion:
It doesn't hurt to be a good citizen, whether or not you know how to drive well.

Driving the Big One

Later, when she is in the U. S. Army Reserves, Mommy was required to get a military license. To understand how it was that Mommy actually got licensed, you have to understand that Mommy is gullible. She misses details that would point out inconsistencies and tip her off that she is being had. Getting her military license is a good example of that.

When Mommy first joined her reserve unit, she was told that she needed to have a military license and that she should be tested to drive the biggest vehicle in the swamp. (The swamp is not a pool of water; it is a motor pool.) Mommy believed what she was told.

"Can you drive stick shift?" asked the sergeant in charge of the swamp.

"Certainly," said Mommy. "I learned to drive on a tractor." (That probably explains her problems with parallel parking and angle parking. I have never seen a tractor parallel parked or angle parked in our town.)

"Good," said the sergeant. "I can bring you a larger vehicle then. I'll be right back."

He drove up with a 2 1/2–ton oil tanker, called by the people in the swamp a "deuce-and-a-half." Mommy looked at that and thought about how she could drive something like that. The step was over her head, so she knew she would not be able to see out the window. She could not see out the window in our van, either. She had to use pillows. Ah, ha! She had a solution.

71

"Give me just a minute," she told the swamp sergeant. "I'll be right back."

She ran to the parking lot and returned to the oil tanker with the pillows from our van. The sergeant was waiting for her, and he helped her climb into the cab by pushing her up.

Mommy fluffed her pillows into place, and then started the oil tanker. The swamp sergeant told her where to go. They drove around the military compound. Mommy found out that she did not need her pillows. In order to turn the wheel, she had to stand up and hang on it, using her body weight, not her arm strength, to turn it. So, she drove standing up.

Pretty soon, she and the swamp sergeant were dizzy from driving in circles. The swamp sergeant decided that they needed an adventure, and he told Mommy to drive out of the compound. They drove down the road a little bit.

"Okay," he said. "Just turn right here." "Here" was McKnight Road, a major thoroughfare through Pittsburgh.

Wow," thought Mommy. "I hope all the people out on the road are going to watch out for me." She did not have to worry. She was the biggest vehicle on the road, so, of course, the other ones watched out for her.

Finally, she was allowed to turn around and drive back to the military compound. There, everyone was waiting for her at the entrance.

"Just parallel park it over there," the swamp sergeant pointed to a very little spot. That was when Mommy figured out that the swamp was playing a joke on her. The joke was really on them, though, because they had to give Mommy a license to drive anything up to and including a deuce-and-a-half.

As for me, I say "Watch out, world! Mommy is really licensed now!"

Conclusion:
Chutzpah will take you many places,
including down McKnight Road in a deuce-and-a-half.

Washing Cars and Clothes, Needed or Not

Mommy is not the only one who drives. Sometimes Daddy drives the car, too. Often, when Daddy drives, Mommy is in the passenger seat.

Daddy is a good driver. He is an even better car owner. He takes good care of the car. He gets the oil changed all the time, and he takes the car through the car wash.

Mommy and I like to go to the car wash with him. It is fun to watch all the machines clean our car.

One time when Mommy and I went with Daddy, the machines did more than wash the car. They also washed Mommy's skirt. She found that out when she went to get out of the car at the store. Part of her skirt was wet—the part that she shut in the door and that was hanging out at the car wash. (Mommy sure has problems with skirts.)

Mommy also has problems with car washes. She sometimes goes to them herself, without Daddy. Boy, is that a mistake!

One time she went to a car wash in Salinas, California, where Daddy works. She drove up to the car wash, but she could not get into it because the wheel got stuck. The green light kept telling her to go, but she could not move. Usually there are lots of people behind her. This time there was no one, and the gas station attendants were both busy and far away. Mommy was afraid to leave the car because the automatic track kept trying to pull it—only the car wasn't going anywhere. Finally, Mommy got out and gave the car a big shove. Magic! The track grabbed the car and started pulling it into the car wash—only no one was inside the car! Mommy had to run fast to get into the car before the water hit it and her.

Sometimes Mommy is not as lucky with car washes as she was in Salinas. One time she was in Champaign, Illinois. She had just driven all the way there after work from Bloomington, Indiana (three hours). My sister lives there, and Mommy was going to visit for the weekend. However, when she drove up to my sister's apartment, no one heard her ring the buzzer to get it because my sister was having a party. Mommy could see that through the window. So, Mommy called my sister on the phone, but there was only a message, saying that no one was available to talk to her. But Mommy could see my sister in the window!

Even though Mommy was very tired, she decided to go get the car washed before starting to throw rocks at my sister's window because the car, which belonged to my sister, was quite dirty from the trip. Mommy drove up to the car wash and into it—no problems this time. Then, my Mommy waited for the car to be washed, but she was, indeed, very, very tired. Watching the car wash machines must be a lot like watching television for Mommy because quite soon she toppled over, sound asleep. When she did that, she hit the window switch. All of a sudden, the window was wide open, and the car was being washed both inside and out. Mommy was being washed, too, and by the time she got the window back up (after a lot of surprised fumbling), she had also got all her clothes washed—without even having to remove them.

Conclusion:
Too great a fascination with machines
makes you forget to think.

MOMMY'S TRANSPORTATION TRIBULATIONS

Shenan (CB) Leaver (with Betty Lou Leaver)

Trouble with Cars

Maybe it has something to do with being detail-oblivious, or maybe it has more to do with simple absent-mindedness, but Mommy sometimes forgets things. She often forgets things that are related to cars. Let me tell you a story about that.

My sister and Mommy used to share a car. Sometimes my mommy would drive my sister to work, and then go on to work herself. She would have to pick up my sister after work. Other times, or times when Mommy was going to work late, my sister would drop Mommy off and then pick her up when she called.

Unfortunately, one evening when Mommy called to be picked up, my sister did not answer. In fact, no one answered. Everyone was away from home.

Mommy had no choice. She settled in and started to work on some projects that needed to be done, waiting until someone showed up at home, realized that she was not back yet, and called her. One hour went by, then two, then three. Finally, she called again. Surely by 9:00 someone would have returned home, but no, we were all busy with school and other activities.

Poor Mommy! She sat and worked and waited some more. A little while later, one of her assistants came in. He sat and chatted. After a half-hour or so, he asked Mommy why she was working so late. She explained about the car and no one being home.

"But, Ma'am," her assistant said, "I just saw your car. It's parked in the parking lot."

Lucky Mommy! If her assistant had not come in, she might have been there all night.

Another assistant, when he heard the story, told Mommy that she was not the only one to have car troubles. One morning he woke up, and his car was missing. He panicked and called the police. He was lucky. They found his car. It was in a parking garage downtown. Then he remembered. He had driven to town and taken the bus home. Oops!

Mommy's secretary, Jacqueline, had car trouble, too. One day her truck would not start when she was at work. She called the repair shop, and they sent a tow truck. She gave them a key to the truck and told them where it was parked. In an hour or so, the shop called to say that the key did not work. She could not understand that. It worked for her. She asked a colleague to take her to the shop. As they walked to the colleague's car, she saw her truck sitting where she had left it. The repair shop had towed away someone else's truck.

Conclusion:
Sometimes bosses have a bad influence on their employees.

More Trouble with Cars

Mommy does not have trouble just with cars that are standing still. Mommy figures that if something can go wrong, plan that it will.

When she was a lieutenant in the reserves in Pittsburgh, her unit had to go to training a long way away in New York. Mommy volunteered to drive her van because the unit needed a vehicle for bringing some of the large-size supplies. Everyone else was driving jeeps.

So, Mommy and one of the captains put the unit's equipment in the van and joined the caravan of military vehicles. For a long time, they followed all the jeeps that were moving slowly along the interstate.

After a while, they got tired of the slow driving, so they moved to the head of the line. As Mommy drove by, the captain rolled down the window and serenaded each vehicle they passed, singing "Strangers in the night...."

Mommy and he felt pretty good about the good time that they were making. They had already left the slow-moving caravan behind, and they made plans for arriving early and getting the tents and other supplies set up. They were going to be very popular when everyone else got there and found half their work all done.

Soon they saw a sign. They were leaving Syracuse and heading into an unpopulated north. They should be at Fort Drum in another hour or so, they figured. Yes! They were very pleased.

Then something happened. They heard a loud noise, and the van started wobbling. Oh, oh! Mommy had blown a tire.

They stopped to change the tire. The spare was under all the equipment. The captain and Mommy took out all the equipment and put it on the roadside. Then, they pulled out the spare tire. It was flat.

The captain walked down the road to hitch a ride into the nearest town, where he could call AAA. My mommy put the equipment back in the van and waited for his return.

In a couple of hours, he was back with a tow truck. Off they went to the repair station. A couple of hours later, they were on their way.

When they arrived, the whole unit was there. They were just sitting, waiting to sing *Strangers in the Night* to them. They had not been able to do anything while they were waiting because Mommy and the captain had all their stuff.

Mommy parked the van, and everyone got his or her stuff out. They spent a whole week at Fort Drum. At the end of the week, they put their stuff back into the van and made a caravan to go back to Pittsburgh. This time, Mommy was at the end.

The caravan started up. The caravan drove off. Mommy just sat there.

"What's wrong?" asked the captain.

"The van won't start," Mommy said sadly.

The captain said it was *déjà vu*: another phone found, another AAA call, another tow truck, another repair job, and arrival long after everyone else was home. This time, though, they did not have a chance to sing *Strangers in the Night* to anyone. Mommy said it was life as usual.

Conclusion:
One person's trouble is another person's trifle.

Teaching My Sister To Drive While Cowering under the Seat

Daddy was away from home, when my sister turned 16, so Mommy taught her to drive. That was a mistake.

My sister said it was not very encouraging to have Mommy cowering under the seat, muttering, "We're all going to die," while trying to teach her to drive. Somehow, though, she did learn to drive.

First, Mommy took her on a back road, where there were almost no other cars. That made my sister feel better. They practiced there for a while; then Mommy said they should go home and go out again the next day. After that, she would teach my sister how to drive on the main road through town.

"Just turn left here," she said to my sister, "and we'll sneak home on back roads." That was a mistake. My sister turned — onto the main drag through town.

The next time they went out, my sister drove the main roads and the back roads. She was getting pretty good. Mommy told her that after a little more practice, she would show her how to drive on a freeway and teach her how to merge.

"Just turn left here," she said, "and we'll go home."

"But Mom," protested my sister. "That is an entrance ramp to Route 66."

"No," answered my Mom. "It just looks like the entrance ramp to route 66. It's really a suburban road with an entrance ramp. There will not be any cars here, so you will get a chance to see how merging works without having to merge." That was a mistake. My sister turned left—onto the entrance ramp to Route 66.

My sister must be a slow learner. She kept letting Mommy teach her. Daddy says that he was glad he did not know that Mommy was teaching my sister to drive.

One of the last times that Mommy was helping sister, right before she got her license, my sister was pretty confident about driving. She drove along at speed limit in the left lane, with both windows down, on a very pretty, autumn day. She was doing very well, except that Mommy wanted her to change lanes so that she could make a right turn. Mommy needed her to slow down and get behind a convertible that was in the right lane right beside her.

"Slow down," Mommy said, but my sister must not have heard her. She did not respond, and the time for changing lanes was running out.

"Slow down," Mommy yelled. The car in the right-hand lane screeched to a stop.

Conclusion:
When giving orders, make sure they go to the right person.

Trouble on Foot

Mommy identifies cars not by make but by color. She does know the difference between station wagons, trucks, vans, and cars. However, she does not notice any smaller categories than that, except for color. Thus, there are green station wagons and brown station wagons, blue trucks and white trucks, brown vans and black vans, and red cars and white cars. If someone tells her the make of a car, she never will recognize it. She needs to know the color.

Mommy always parks our car underneath a light. That way, she can always find it, and she always knows which blue car is ours.

Once Mommy's friend, Katie, who drives a white truck, offered to pick up Mommy after work. Mommy had been in Katie's truck a number of times. So, she knew what the truck looked like. That was easy: it was white.

Katie told Mommy to meet her at 4:00 at a corner near the bank where Mommy was going to be. Katie was going to be in a hurry, and at that hour in Arlington, Virginia, where Mommy was living at the time, there would be a lot of traffic. Katie thought that it would be hard to make the turn into the bank from the direction she would be coming from because of all the rush-hour traffic. So they made plans for Mommy to come to the road on the non-parking-lot side of the bank. That way she could just jump into the truck when Katie drove up.

For once, Mommy was on time. She was standing on the

corner when the white truck drove up exactly at 4:00 and stopped at the red light. In hopped Mommy.

"Hi," she said, turning to talk to Katie. However, instead of her friend, there was a very surprised-looking man sitting behind the wheel.

"Oops!" said Mommy. "Wrong truck." With that, she hopped back out, as the light turned green.

Conclusion:
Color is not the most important characteristic.

All Aboard

I do not know how to explain Mommy's train trouble. All trains are the same color, so I guess they are even harder to tell apart than cars, which, at least, come in different colors. The different colors really do help Mommy, and we have proof of that.

One day Mommy was going from Charlottesville, Virginia, where she was staying with friends, to Washington, D.C., where she was working. It is a short, easy train trip between the two cities.

The train was late, however, and Mommy was concerned about getting to work on time. Finally, the train pulled in. Thank goodness!

Passengers got out; then, the conductor yelled out "All aboard." All the waiting people surged onto the train. Mommy jumped on with a sigh of relief, figuring that she would be able to make it to work with nary a minute to spare.

The train began moving. "First stop," said the conductor, and he named some city that Mom had never heard of. She wondered how that could be. She had taken the train a number of times between Washington, D.C. and Charlottesville, and she knew all the cities along the way.

An hour later, she found out why she had not recognized the name of the next city. The train was headed south, not north! Mommy had boarded on the wrong train.

Mommy got out at the next stop. There she waited for more than two hours, until a train headed for Washington, D.C. finally showed up. Mommy was not only late for work that day, she missed it entirely.

That's my mommy. She misses little details most of the time and big details sometimes.

Conclusion:
It takes a long time to reach the North when you head south.

UP IN THE AIR
AND
AROUND THE
WORLD
WITH MOMMY

Shenan (CB) Leaver (with Betty Lou Leaver)

A Questionable Heritage

There is something about Mommy and England that just does not mesh. However, Mommy says that she is of British lineage and that our ancestors came to the United States from England on a famous boat called *The Mayflower*. One would not know that judging by Mommy. Well, here, you judge.

The first time that Mommy went to England on a business trip, she arrived at the Philadelphia airport, after having done a couple of weeks of work in Philadelphia en route. The ticket agent asked Mommy for her passport.

"What do I need a passport for?" asked Mommy.

"Because you are going to a foreign country," the agent replied.

"No, I'm not," Mommy told her. "I'm going to England."

"England is a foreign country," the agent responded.

"How can that be?" asked Mommy. "They speak English there."

Poor Mommy! The agent would not let her on the plane. Mommy called home, and my brother found her passport. He sent it to her on the next flight from our town, but it got lost on the way. Mommy spent a long time in Philadelphia.

Finally, the airlines found the passport, and Mommy was allowed to go to England. When she arrived, she found that England really was a foreign country. The airport looked very different from out airports, and the signs say different things. One sign on a long, strange-looking corridor said "Way Out."

Mommy thought, "Wow! That really is way out!" Then, she realized that it was supposed to be an exit sign.

Then Mommy came to the passport control and immigration agent. The woman asked her something. Mommy did not understand. The woman repeated, and Mommy still did not understand. Then, the agent asked something else, and Mommy did not understand.

"You're from America, and you don't speak English?" the agent asked in exasperation. That question Mommy did understand.

"No, I do not speak English," Mommy explained. "I speak American." Clearly, there is a difference.

Mommy had a lot of trouble communicating in England after she made it past the immigration folks. They talked in very funny ways, and it was not just the different accent.

One colleague told her that he was shortsighted. "Don't be so hard on yourself," Mommy told him, not realizing that he only meant that he was near-sighted.

"Where should I put these books? They are a little hard to carry," Mommy asked another colleague, when they came out of a bookstore. She was quite surprised by the answer.

"If you want," she replied, "you can put them in your boot." Mommy stared at her incredulously. How on earth were her books going to fit into her boot? And why would anyone want to put them there, anyway? After a short discussion, Mommy realized that her colleague was suggesting that Mommy put the books into the trunk of her rental car. Later, she found out that the hood of the car is called a bonnet. I guess people in England think cars are people: they wear bonnets and boots.

The mistakes were not only informal. Sometimes they were formal. While in England, Mommy had to make a presentation on teaching in the United States. People listened very politely, and Mommy thought that they were understanding her. Then, one participant asked her about American teachers' credentials for teaching.

"Oh," said Mommy. "Most American teachers are certified."

A clap of thunder resounded throughout the room. Mommy quickly recognized it as hysterical laughter. Someone who spoke American and English, told Mommy that she had just announced that most American teachers are crazy.

I do not believe all those stories about *The Mayflower*. I would think that someone whose family was from England would know better how to behave there and how to talk there.

Conclusion:
Lineage does not always explain who we are.

Shenan (CB) Leaver (with Betty Lou Leaver)

Not a Terrorist

There is another reason that Mommy does not have good memories of England. One time when she was there, she just went for three days to a conference. She came one day, gave a talk the next day, and left on the third day.

At least, she tried to leave on the third day, but that was easier said than done. Apparently, there was a bomb threat on the plane, and the bobbies in England were questioning all the passengers very carefully. All of the passengers except Mommy passed the screening.

Mommy could answer all the questions with words that the bobbies wanted to hear except for one: "Where are your other suitcases?" Mommy had come with only a carry-on bag—she was only going to be there three days, so she did not think that she would need more than that.

The bobbies did not want to believe her. "No one crosses the Atlantic with only a carry-on," they told her.

She explained that overworked globe-trotting mothers who try to make their lives as simple as possible, since there is no way that their lives could ever possibly be made easy, do. The bobbies did not believe her.

The bobbies made Mommy sit in an interrogation room for a half-hour. When she was unable to produce any additional suitcases, they thought that she was unwilling to produce one. Finally, they called in someone in charge, and he let Mommy go. He said that she was no terrorist, just a crazy American.

That experience did not endear Mommy to England. More-over, she had just come to London to the airport from Leeds, where she had expected to buy a bus ticket. However, because the bus left at midnight, the ticket office was closed. Mommy had to bribe the bus driver to let her on the bus—which had no bathroom. Mommy figured she could get out at a rest stop, but, as it turned out, the drivers changed at the rest stop, and the driver she had bribed told her not to leave the bus because she would not be able to get back on.

By the time Mommy left the bus in London, she was in a lot of physical pain. By the time she left the airport in London, she was in a lot of psychological pain. Poor Mommy! She should have taken a ticket and two suitcases.

Conclusion:
If you do not want to be mistaken for a terrorist,
don't look or act like one.

Ticket Trouble

Mommy travels a lot, so you would think that she would learn how to handle airports and tickets — but she does not. I guess she is a slow learner, like teachers call me. She keeps making mistakes about which airport to go to, when to go, and where her ticket is.

Very recently, she had flown into Reagan National Airport in Washington, DC without incident. Wow! A first! She was so pleased. When she returned, she went to the airport early. That was a first, too. She usually runs in at the last minute. She was so proud. Moreover, there was no line as she walked up to the counter to get the boarding pass for her electronic ticket.

"I am on your noon flight to Phoenix," she told the ticket agent.

"That cannot be," the ticket agent replied. "We have no noon flight to Phoenix."

"But," Mommy protested, "You must have. I have a noon flight listed on my itinerary." She handed the itinerary to the ticket agent.

The ticket agent looked at the itinerary, then looked at Mommy rather strangely. "Ma'am," he said, pointing with his finger, "You do have a noon flight, but not from here. It is from Baltimore-Washington International Airport." Oops!

Another time, Mommy ended up at Sheremetovo Airport in Moscow just in time for her 9:00 p.m. flight. She filled out her declaration form and slipped through the customs line with no trouble at all. She was very pleased. She was on time, and she had a ticket in her hand. She was definitely at the right airport because it was the only airport with flights to Helsinki, her destination. She walked up to the ticket counter, quite pleased. It was a rare occasion when she did not have some problem to deal with. The ticket agent looked at her strangely and said, "Ma'am, this flight departed six hours ago."

Mommy did not understand. She showed the agent the itinerary where it showed a 9:00 flight. The agent showed her the ticket where it said 3:00. Who would have thought! The agent explained that one has to fly by the ticket, not by the itinerary. Then, she saw Mommy's name and realized that the airline had permanently lost Mommy's luggage on the way there. She wanted to help Mommy, but the flight was full. She told Mommy that she could sit in one of the stewardess's jump seats because they had an extra one of those. Mommy agreed. After all, she had no luggage to worry about.

That, of course, was a little better than the time Mommy arrived at Domodedovo Airport in Moscow, en route to Siberia. She looked and looked for her ticket, but it was nowhere to be found. Oops! That was a problem because she did not have very much money with her. In fact, she had just enough money to buy a one-way ticket to Siberia. She figured she could somehow get back from Krasnoyarsk, the city she was going to in Siberia, and she did—by trading books for a ticket.

A one-way ticket to Siberia was something that Mommy got a lot of times. Mommy really likes to travel to Siberia. She likes it so much that she will even go on a one-way ticket. Some people get sent to Siberia, or at least they did in the old days, which weren't all that long ago. That was a different kind of one-way ticket, but my mommy is not at all worried about getting stuck there.

Once, with my sister, she went to Akademgorodok in Siberia on a one-way ticket deliberately. She figured she could get a ticket back while she was there. So, one day she and my sister took the bus from Akademgorodok to the airport. Everything worked out well, and Mommy soon had return tickets. She went outside to catch the bus back, but there was no bus stop to Akademgorodok. She asked some people about that. Yes, they told her, the bus comes here from there, but it does not return. Mommy is sure a one-way Mommy!

Another time she was at the airport in Kemerovo in Siberia with my brother. She was very proud of herself because she had gone to Kemerovo on a roundtrip ticket.

"This is the first time I've been in Siberia with a return ticket," she bragged to my brother.

He looked at the ticket and said, "Don't be so sure, Mom. This ticket is for yesterday." Poor Mommy! She just cannot get out of Siberia very easily. (She says that Siberia has always been a difficult place to leave.

Conclusion:
Before you leave home, make sure you have your ticket,
but if you do not have it, go, anyway. It may be an interesting
experience.

Shenan (CB) Leaver (with Betty Lou Leaver)

Trouble with Travels

It is not just tickets that Mommy has trouble with. She also has trouble with planes and all kinds of travel. Maybe it is because of the kinds of places to which she travels. Sometimes, even ticket agents cannot find these places on a map.

Once Mommy was flying to Moldova, which is a country that used to belong to the Soviet Union but is now independent. It is to the east of Romania, and not very many airlines fly there. So, Mommy had to fly Moldovan Airlines. When she was about to get on a plane from Moscow to Moldova, part of the plane's propeller fell on the runway right near where she was standing. Some man emerged from inside the plane and told people that they were having a little trouble at the moment. Mommy very quickly figured out what the "little trouble" was.

Another time Mommy was consulting in Bukhara, Uzbekistan, which is on the boarder of Uzbekistan and Tajikistan in Central Asia. Uzbekistan is another of those countries that people have trouble finding on the map and that were part of the former Soviet Union. Not very many Americans go there because you have to be able to speak either Uzbek or Russian, but Mommy goes there a lot. Usually she has few travel problems, but once it took her six days to get from Bukhara to Houston, Texas.

People told her not to take Bukhara Air, but she did not listen. She took the flight from Bukhara to Tashkent on Bukhara Air—and it was a perfect flight. She stayed overnight in Tashkent and got up in the morning to take another airlines from Tashkent to Moscow, en route to New York City and Houston. Unfortunately, that plane had fallen apart en route to Tashkent, so there was no plane to use to get people to Moscow. That is Mommy's kind of luck: planes falling apart.

Mommy stayed in Tashkent two more days. Then, when she did get a flight out, she had to talk her way past the border guards in Moscow because she no longer had a valid ticket from Moscow out of the country and no visa for Moscow. That is Mommy's kind of luck: no visa when it is needed.

After making it into Moscow, Mommy stayed a couple of days until she could get a flight to New York City. The flight, when she finally got it, was uneventful.

Mommy was now feeling rather fortunate. She should not have been.

In New York City, she got on the flight to Houston and relaxed. She should not have. Bam! The plane shook. Mommy knew what had happened because she had felt this sensation once in leaving Houston, when the baggage-loading vehicle ran into the side of the plane and damaged the baggage door. This time the food truck servicing the plane had run into it and put a hole into its side. Now it could not fly. Everyone had to get off and take a plane through Atlanta to Houston. That is Mommy's kind of luck: Planes getting damaged by loading vehicles running into them.

There was a man in the waiting area for the Atlanta flight. He overheard Mommy telling someone that this was her sixth day, trying to get to Houston from Uzbekistan. He listened to everything that had happened to Mommy. Then he got up and walked over to the gate agent.

"I would like a different flight," he told the agent.

"Yes, sir," she replied. "What flight would you like?"

"Any flight that *she* is not on," he said, pointing to Mommy.

The agent laughed, but the man did not. He made the agent put him on a different flight.

Mommy seems to have a bad influence on the travels of

people around her. So, perhaps the man was right to get on a different plane. I can give you a couple of examples.

Mommy's sister, my Aunt Valerie, was traveling to see us when she was 15. At the time, she was living with my grandmother in Maine, and we were living in Washington, D.C. Grandma took Aunt Valerie to the airport and waved to her as she boarded the plane. However, she never showed up in Washington. Mommy looked and looked. The she had the airlines page Aunt Valerie. When the airlines learned that Aunt Valerie was only 15, they searched real hard for her. They found her, too — in Columbia, South Carolina. Since she was coming to the District of Columbia, she felt that it made sense to get on a plane headed for Columbia.

A different kind of travel problem happened to one of Mommy's students. A very nice but absent-minded lady once took a course that Mommy was teaching. She came all the way from Japan to take the course. Mommy tried to tell her that it is cold on the Central Coast of California in the summer time, but I guess she did not believe Mommy because she brought a lot of summer clothes with her. She could not wear the summer clothes because it really was too cold. So, she thought that she would make her travels easier by mailing the clothes to her home address in Japan. That did not make things easier for her, though, because she left her passport in the pocket of her shorts. Oops! Goodbye, passport! Mommy, of course, is used to passport troubles, so she helped her student get a replacement passport fast.

Conclusion:
If you want an easy time traveling, avoid Mommy! If you want excitement, tag along!

Shenan (CB) Leaver (with Betty Lou Leaver)

Fun with Luggage

Mommy does not only have trouble with tickets and planes. She also has trouble with luggage. It does not always end up where she is, or she puts wrong things into it, or it disappears.

The first time that Mommy had trouble with luggage was on a trip from Los Angeles to Moscow via Helsinki on Finnair. When Mommy got to Moscow, her luggage was nowhere to be found. It never did show up. Mommy said it vanished into Finnair.

The next time Mommy lost luggage, it was only for a short period of time. Mommy flew from Prague to Monterey, but her luggage flew from Prague to Moscow. Mommy figured that those M-cities must sound alike or look alike to baggage handlers.

Another time Mommy and Daddy went to Florida and took their kayak with them. They put the paddles into a golf bag and tied it with a tarp. When the bag did not show up, the customer service representative asked them to pick out the kind of bag that was missing from a book of pictures. There was nothing like their bag there!

Mommy also gets into trouble with luggage because of what she puts into it. Once she packed a bottle of wine in her bag, thinking to hand carry it. At the last minute, she forgot and checked the bag. The wine came through great.

However, some other guy must have done the same thing with less luck because when Mommy flew from the Ukraine (another one of those former Soviet Union countries) to Middlebury, Vermont, where she was teaching a summer semester course, her bag was underneath that man's suitcase (actually, a vinyl balg-like suitcase), which had been packed full of vodka. The vodka bottles had broken and leaked into Mommy's suitcase. All her clothes were soaked with vodka. When Mommy finally got to the college in the middle of the night, after a series of delayed plane flights, the laundry room was locked. All she could do was dry out her clothes. She had to teach a class before the laundry room opened, so she went to class reeking of vodka. If she wanted to make an impression, she probably did!

The worst time was when Mommy brought back a jar of bryusnika, little red cranberries from Siberia. She carried the jar carefully in hand-luggage from Siberia to Moscow and from Moscow to Munich, then put it into the suitcase which she deposited into Left Luggage at the Munich Airport because she was just taking her packpack for a short trip on the train down to Innsbruck, Austria, to visit her friends, Martina and Andreas. Coming back, she took a van, which arrived very late at the airport, and she had to run and grab her left-luggage to get onto the plane for New York and then California. She forgot all about the jar being in her suitcase. When the bag arrived home, everything was all red: clothes, books, and Mommy's presents for us. (The red did not wash out, either.) Mommy just washed everything off, and to this day we have some red reminders on our bookshelves and in Mommy's closet of that trip.

Conclusion:
Just figure that with luggage what goes in
is not necessarily what comes out.

Meeting People in Boston

One of the things Mommy does to make an income is write books. This means that Mommy occasionally has to go somewhere to meet with a potential publisher. So, when Mommy was teaching that summer in Middlebury, Vermont, she made an appointment with Harry, a representative of a Boston-area publisher for a book she was working on.

Apparently, this was to be one of those memorable meetings—memorable because of all the things that went wrong. Part of it was Mommy's bad luck—that seems to happen a lot, and part of it was that Mommy failed to get all the details she needed about the trip—that seems to happen a lot, too.

The first detail that Mommy missed was the weather report for the day in question. It was a long walk to the bus station, but it was mostly downhill. It would have been okay, except that it rained very hard that day. Worst, Mommy overslept, so she ended up jogging to the bus station with a computer in her backpack in the pouring rain. That slowed her down a little and made her out of breath a lot.

The second detail that Mommy missed was the location of the bus station. Actually, she knew where the bus station was and went there—but it was the wrong bus station. She wondered how on earth there could be two bus stations in a town half the size of Podunk.

Mommy ran over to the other bus station—literally. She knew she had missed her bus, but she thought there might be another one that could get her to Boston on time.

As it turned out, her bus had not yet showed up. Mommy was happy. She should not have been. That was not a good sign. The bus finally came, and every town it came to on the way to Boston, it got later and later. Mommy's bus pulled into Boston very late.

The third mistake Mommy made was in not getting a telephone number where she could call Harry if problems developed. All she knew was the name and address of the hotel restaurant near the bus station where they planned to meet. She ran from the bus station to the hotel, hoping that he would still be there.

When Mommy walked in the door, she realized her fourth mistake. She had forgotten to ask Harry what he looked like. There were lots of men in that hotel restaurant. Mommy went from one to another, asking, "Are you Harry?"

One man she asked stood up and said, "I could be if you would like me to be." Mommy decided that she would not like him to be.

Mommy did find Harry eventually. She also met a lot of other people whom she had not planned to meet.

Conclusion:
There are better ways to win friends and influence people than to ask people if they are Harry.

MOMMY
ON THE FARM

Shenan (CB) Leaver (with Betty Lou Leaver)

Starting Young

Mommy's problems with details and not quite getting things right started when she was a kid in the country. Not everything went right there, either.

Where Mommy grew up in Maine it snowed a lot. So, when it started to snow, people would head home. One day my grandpa noticed that it was going to snow, so he left work and headed home. On the way, he picked up Mommy at her school in a nearby town. He did not leave soon enough, however, and the snow started while they were still leaving town. Once they were in the country and the foothills to the White Mountains, the snowstorm turned into a blizzard. The road got very, very slippery. Grandpa drove very, very slowly, but he could not see the ice because it was underneath the snow. The road made a sharp turn, but Grandpa did not. The car slid off the road. Grandpa could not get it out of the ditch, so he told Mommy to wait in the car and he would fetch the nearest neighbor, Donald Gates, who lived a couple of miles down the road.

While Mommy was waiting, a man appeared outside her window. Mommy was afraid. She did not want to open the window. Grandma had always told her not to talk to strangers. The man was insistent, however, so Mommy rolled down the window just a crack.

"Do you need some help?" asked the man.

"No," said Mommy. "My daddy went to get Donald Gates."

"Then I had better wait with you," said the man.

"Oh, no," said Mommy, who was now alarmed. "You don't have to do that. Donald Gates lives really, really close. He and Daddy will be here any minute."

The man insisted on waiting, no matter what Mommy said. Mommy rolled up the window really tight and tried to ignore him. Where was Grandpa? she worried. When would he get back?

After a while, Grandpa finally appeared. Mommy was really relieved, even though he was alone. Now he would get rid of that man. Grandpa came close, and Mommy rolled down the window. Then, Grandpa did something unexpected. He held out his hand to the strange man.

"Hi, Donald," he said. "I was just looking for you."

"So your daughter told me," the strange man answered.

Conclusion:
Sometimes help is closer than you think it is
and looks different from what you think it does.

Fishing for Men

Mommy really did grow up on a farm. It was located in the mountains of Maine, not far from the ocean. In that part of Maine there are many good ponds and excellent fishing streams. Everyone there fishes for hornpout.

Once, a couple of boys who went to school with Mommy and her sister invited them to come fishing with them. They took their fishing rods and a sack lunch and went to their friends' house.

At their friends' house, they climbed into two canoes, my Mom's sister, Karen, with Danny and Mommy with Jimmy. They spent the morning casting for fish and paddling the river that ran through Danny and Jimmy's parents' property.

By noon, they had not caught anything yet, but they still had time. They pulled the canoes up on shore side by side and sat on the riverbank. They ate their sack lunches. (Grandma had made the lunches, so they were edible.)

After lunch, they had much better luck. Everyone, that is, except Mommy. Karen caught a couple hornpout, and so did Danny. Mommy thought that maybe their canoe was in a better place in the river, but Jimmy was catching fish, too.

Jimmy told Mommy that she was not very good at casting. So, he showed her how to do it better. Mommy thought that she understood. She took the fishing pole back and did what Jimmy had shown her. The reel spun, and the line, with the hook for the fish, went flying through the air. Mommy could not see where it went, but she immediately felt that she had caught something really big. She started to really it in.

Jimmy was excited, too. He was shouting. Mommy could not hear him very well because she was concentrating on reeling in her catch. Finally she heard him.

"Stop!" he yelled. "Stop. Stop now."

Mommy did not at first understand why he wanted her to stop. Then she saw what had happened, at the same time that Jimmy explained.

"Stop! It's not a fish! You caught me!"

Mommy's hook was twisted into his t-shirt. It took Jimmy's Mom twenty minutes to get it out.

I have heard people say that sometimes women fish for men. I've also heard other people talking someone being a good catch. I did not understand what the expression really meant until my aunt told me about Mommy's fishing trip.

Conclusion:
Catching a person is not the same as catching a fish.

A Farmer in Leningrad

Mommy, the farmer's daughter, grew up to work in a profession that required her to live in the city. It also required her to do some fancy things once in a while.

Once Mommy and my sister were in St. Petersburg, Russia. (Back then, it was called Leningrad.) Mommy and my sister were visiting the Consul General at the U.S. Consulate there, and they were the guests of honor at breakfast.

Mommy and my sister talked with everyone around the table. The guests chatted, as the maid placed an eggcup with an egg in front of each person's plate.

Mommy did not know what to do with the egg in the eggcup. She thought about it, as she continued to talk, and she still could not figure it out. There was not an obvious way to handle it. She watched what the others were doing. What they were doing was waiting for her, the guest of honor, to start eating before they did. Here was a dilemma. Mommy kept talking, hoping that someone would get hungry enough to start eating, but none did. That is the way it is with diplomats. They have to be polite.

Finally, Mommy was very hungry, and she figured everyone else was, too. She decided to do a very brave thing. She would eat her egg as she was used to eating it. She seized the egg, dragged it out of the eggcup onto her plate, and smashed it with a knife.

The egg was very soft. It made a very big mess on Mommy's plate.

Everyone else then gently tapped open their eggs with a spoon and scooped out the egg bit by bit, eating it. My sister did that, too, as she whispered to Mommy, "I don't think you were supposed to kill the egg with a knife."

Poor Mommy! She was not able to eat very much of that egg, so she was very hungry after breakfast.

She was also embarrassed, but she was used to that. She had learned over time that things are done differently in the country and the city.

Her first embarrassing high society incident occurred while she was at college. Her best friend, Eileen, invited her to Philadelphia. There Eileen's family took the two of them to a very expensive restaurant for dinner. Mommy dressed up as best as she could, and she was on her very best behavior. At least, she tried to be.

She did not like soup, however, and had never been able to force herself to eat it. (That was very strange for a farm girl, where soup is a staple, but that is the way it was then with Mommy.) She would not have ordered soup for herself, but Eileen's father ordered a full dinner for everyeone, and that included soup. Oh, well, Mommy decided she would tryu to swallow and say nothing about not liking it. After all, that is what she was taught that good social behavior was all about.

So, when the waiter brought her a huge bowl of warm liquid, she picked up her soupspoon and enthusiastically started sipping what she considered to be a very tasteless dish.

The waiter looked very confused. "Miss," he said. "This is the finger bowl for washing your hands."

I think Mommy just does not have a good understanding of what various liquids are for. Some you drink; some you use for cleaning; yet others are used for other purposes. Yet, Mommy thinks they have one purpose.

Yeah, there was another incident like this. Daddy told me that when Mommy was giving birth to my sister, the nurse brought in an enema big filled with water. Mommy looked at her in great surprise and told her in all seriousness, "I don't think I can drink all that!"

Conclusion:
You can take the farmer off the farm,
but you cannot take the farm out of the farmer.

Shenan (CB) Leaver (with Betty Lou Leaver)

The Driving Instructor

Since Mommy grew up on a farm, she learned to drive a tractor very young, like many other farmers' children do. Mommy was the oldest of all Grandpa's children, so she was the one who drove the tractor most of the time.

When my aunt Karen, the next-younger child in the family, became old enough to drive, the lot fell to my mommy to teach my aunt how to do that. Mommy was really big by then and an experienced tractor driver. She had already turned thirteen. She took her teaching task seriously, but I guess she did not think of all the details — as usual.

On the driving-learning day, my mommy and my Aunt Karen headed out to the field to practice driving. It was a sunny day — perfect for learning to drive a tractor.

When they got to the field, the old Allis Chalmers 1939 tractor, the one that Grandpa, Grandma, and Mommy drive was right where it had been left on the edge of the rows of corn. It was ready to be driven.

Aunt Karen got up on the seat, and Mommy stood on the ground and shouted instructions to her. Perhaps that was Mommy's first mistake.

Aunt Karen put her foot on the clutch and brake like Mommy instructed. Then Mommy told her to turn on the ignition, and she did that. All was going very well. At least, that's what Mommy and Aunt Karen thought.

Then Mommy told Aunt Karen to put her foot on the gas and to let out the clutch. She did that, and the tractor jumped up and then forward. Oh, my! Mommy told Aunt Karen that this was normal, but that if she were to let out the clutch more slowly, the tractor would not jump as high.

Now Aunt Karen was ready to roll. Mommy told her to practice steering around the edge of the field. Aunt Karen did that. So, all was still going well.

Aunt Karen practiced and practiced. She became good at steering around the field.

Then it was time to go home. "Okay," Mommy told her, "we beter go home now. It's getting late." With that, Mommy started walking back to the house. Perhaps that was Mommy's second mistake.

Aunt Karen followed on the tractor. Almost immediately, she ran across a barbed wire fence.

"Help!" she called. "How do you turn off the tractor?"

Mommy did not hear her. She had walked too fast and was too far ahead. Perhaps that was Mommy's third mistake.

A few minutes later, Mommy looked around. She could not find Aunt Karen. She walked back a little bit, and there she found her—and the tractor—all tangled up in the barbed wire fence.

Aunt Karen had only one thing to say when she saw Mommy. "How do you turn this thing off?" she asked.

At last, Mommy told her.

Conclusion:
Do not start something, unless you know how to stop it.

Red Snow

Once when Mommy got all grown up and we kids had shown up in her life, she decided to take us to the farm to see Grandma. Grandpa had died by then, but some of my aunts and uncles were still living on the farm with Grandma.

After dinner the second day we were there, Grandma decided that she wanted to go to town to find some excitement. One of her neighbors was going to take her. So, she got all fancied up, and pretty soon the neighbor drove into the yard. Grandma rode off with him, and we all waved good-by. We were glad that she was going to go find some excitement.

Mommy and Uncle Wesley did the dishes together after supper. Normally, that would only take a half-hour, but Mommy and Uncle Wesley like to talk. In fact, they really like to talk. They talked for a long time; perhaps two hours or even three.

It got late, and it got dark outside. About that time, Uncle Wesley looked out the window at the snow banks. However, instead of a white snow bank, he saw a red one.

"Oh, my goodness," he said. "I got talking, and I forgot to close the damper on the chimney. We have a chimney fire—or a roof fire—or a house fire."

Mommy came upstairs and got us all out of bed. We had to go outside and stand beside the red snow.

Uncle Wesley called the fire department. Well, actually, he called our neighbor, Dodie. In farm country where Mommy grew up, the fire department was composed of volunteers, and the fire truck was always kept in one of the volunteer's driveways. This time, it was at Dodie's.

Uncle Wesley then tried to put out the fire. It was a long wait for the fire department—a half-hour. By then, Uncle Wesley had everything under control. The firemen went up on the roof, anyway, and they looked into the chimney. They made sure the fire was really out. Then they left.

Soon after, Grandma came home. She said it was boring in town. She had not found excitement.

Then, she asked how our evening went. Mommy told her that Dodie had come to visit—along with the rest of the fire department!

Conclusion:
You do not need to leave the farm to find excitement.

IT COULD ONLY HAPPEN TO MOMMY

Shenan (CB) Leaver (with Betty Lou Leaver)

Lacking the Luck of Ganesha

There is a Hindu god, Ganesha, who is supposed to bring good luck. So, one day when Mommy had the chance to buy a little Ganesha at a museum, she did. She put it on a necklace and wore it to work the next day. I guess she wanted lots of luck.

Well, was that a mistake. Mommy's friends told her that she did not need any help in making things work, that she had something called willpower that took care of that. It seems that they probably were right. Here is what happened that "lucky" day.

Mommy went off to work quite happily, with Ganesha dangling away around her throat. (One of her friends said that maybe Ganesha got dizzy, and that was the problem.)

Mommy's bus did not come, though. She had to wait a long while for the next bus.

Then, she came to the metro station and took the train to her regular stop, the metro station that had the second longest escalator in the city—and the up escalator was out of order. Mommy had to walk up a lot of stairs.

Mommy made it to work all right, although late, and she got a lot of work done, working all day on one special project on the computer. She was very pleased. At the end of the day, however, when she went to store the document, she pushed a very wrong button and lost everything that she had done. The network ad-

123

ministrator said that there was no way to retrieve it and that it was very unusual for something like this to happen. Mommy was no longer pleased.

She then left for home. This time the down escalator at the metro station was not working, and she had to walk down a lot of stairs.

By now, Mommy was very tired. That must have been why she did not notice that the train had passed her stop. Oops!

She got out at the next stop, figuring that she could walk across the platform and take the train one stop back. Unfortunately, that particular station was being repaired. To get to the other side, Mommy had to take two different sets of stairs. Well, she only had to take one, but the first set she chose was closed at the top, and there was no note at the bottom to tell her that. She finally made it to the other side, just as the train pulled out of the station. She had to wait another half-hour for the next train.

Finally, Mommy got back to the previous station, made the right transfer, and reached the metro station where she needed to catch the bus home. However, the last bus had by then already left. She asked one of the other bus drivers if he went near the intersection she needed. He said yes, but it turned out that "near" was a half-mile away. So, she had to walk a half-mile back to that intersection in the dark through a bad part of town, then another half-mile up a hill to get back home.

By then Mommy was beginning to have some doubts about Ganesha. All doubts disappeared, however, when near the intersection, the clouds burst, and a raging thunderstorm started. Mommy had not brought an umbrella, but she always carries a spare rain poncho. She pulled it out of her backpack and put it on.

The water from the poncho, however, dripped onto her high heels as she walked up the hill. What more could go wrong, she wondered? She should not have asked. About a block from the house, one of her shoes fell apart.

She took off her shoes and walked in her stocking feet the last block of the way. That put a hole in her stocking. Mommy did not care about the hole, though. She just wanted to get inside the warm house. She could see that people were in the back; the lights were on and so was the sound.

Mommy reached for her key, but she did not have it. She rang the bell, but no one heard. So, she had to traipse through the side garden and knock on the back window.

When she got inside, Mommy took off her wet clothes. She also took off Ganesha and has not worn the pendant since.

Conclusion:
Don't rely on necklace gods
when your own ingenuity will do.

Shenan (CB) Leaver (with Betty Lou Leaver)

My Mommy Wore Combat Boots

Mommy was a soldier and an Army officer when I was little. I do not remember a lot about what happened then, but I do remember Mommy's stories about the things that happened.

Mommy says that in those days the Army had a hang-up about gender differences. Officers, for the most part, were men, and mommies usually did not wear combat boots. In fact, she says that it was not even a nice thing to say to someone that "your mother wears combat boots." I do not see why it is not nice. It is a simply a fact. If your mother puts on those heavy but comfortable black things every morning, then your mother does wear combat boots, right?

Anyway, Mommy says that she had to change genders, at least on paper, to become an officer. I know that is true because I saw the piece of paper. It says that Congress appointed my mother "an officer and gentleman in the U. S. Army." Wow! I think I will avoid going near Congress. They sound like an awfully powerful group of people!

Mommy said that another time, she had a meeting with a general. All the unit commanders had to meet with this general. He said, "Please be seated, gentlemen." Mommy did not sit down. She did not think that he was talking to her. (Guess she forgot about that piece of paper from Congress.) Another commander, who was her friend, pulled her down. He said that this was not the place to make a stand for women's lib. (I do not think that Mommy was making a stand for women's lib; I think she just forgot about Congress making her a gentleman.)

Yet another time, Mommy arrived at Fort Dix, New Jersey for a training exercise. There were lots of tents so that everyone who was there for training could have a place to sleep. There were seven tents for male soldiers, one tent for female soldiers, and one officer's tent. And then there was Mommy. Where to put the one female officer was a big, important question. Senior officers had to have a special meeting just to find Mommy a bed. They seemed to think that they had two choices: Put Mommy with the women or put Mommy with the (male) officers. Finally, they decided. They put Mommy with the (male) officers.

Mommy says that having kids can have a deleterious effect on one's ability to soldier. I am not sure what deleterious means, but maybe it has to do with getting weird looks. For example, Mommy got weird looks the day she had to report to her new commanding officer, after having taken my sister with her to the bank. It probably had something to do with what the commanding officer saw when Mommy turned around to leave. Stuck on the back of her green Army uniform skirt was a bright red lollipop, where my sister, after taking a few licks, had stored the treasure handed to her at the bank.

Mommy also got weird looks when she met another new commanding officer for the first time. She was signing in for summer reserve duty at Fort Devens, Massachusetts, and I was with her. I was still a baby at the time and was walking around the upstairs in my walker where the sign-in was taking place when I discovered another whole world—a set of interesting rooms, separated from me only by a staircase. Bounce! Bounce! I was on my way to exploring the new world. Mommy's new commander was walking up the stairs, and I bounced right into his arms. At the end of her reserve duty, my mommy got the "Bouncing Baby" award. I am so proud! I helped Mommy get an award!

Another time, when my other sister was very little—I think the old-fashioned word for my sister's age then is "suckling"—Mommy was in officer training in Anniston, Alabama. Daddy would pick up Mommy after training every day, and Mommy would nurse my sister as they drove back to the apartment that Daddy and my sisters shared. (Mommy could not live there; she had to live on post.) Before Mommy left post with Daddy and my baby sister, she would change into civilian clothes in her barracks room. One day, the Military Police stopped Daddy and Mommy. The car had an officer's decal, and they were confused. Daddy did not look like an officer. He was overweight and had a beard. Mommy did not look like an officer. She had long hair and was nursing a baby. They said, there was a bet at the MP barracks about who the officer in the car was.

"So," they asked, "Who is the officer?"

Mommy and Daddy looked at each other and replied at the same time, "The baby!"

They were kidding. I think the MPs knew that. I wonder, though, who won the bet.

Americans are not the only ones who are not used to women officers. The Koreans have a problem, too. Once, years after she left military service, Mommy had a meeting with a colonel from the Korean Army. In the conversation, someone else at the meeting said that Mommy had been a U.S. Army officer. The Korean colonel was surprised. He was so surprised that he did not say anything for a long time. As it turned out, he was not only surprised, he was also embarrassed that someone would tell him this. Finally, looking down, he said quietly, "Yes, I understand. Women can be very good at getting secrets out of men."

Mommy did not like that much. She said he did not understand even though he said he did understand.

Conclusion:
Mommies who wear combat boots
should be prepared for people who do not understand.

Shenan (CB) Leaver (with Betty Lou Leaver)

Mommy's Special Weapon

When we lived in Pittsburgh, we had two parts to our house. One part was in a separate apartment, and that is where Daddy had his photography studio and office.

Daddy put an alarm on his office. Although we lived in a nice neighborhood where things were pretty safe, Daddy had lots of expensive photography equipment that he wanted to protect.

There was something strange about that alarm. It was on the same frequency as some other signal, but Daddy could never figure out what that was. So, about once a week, we had to put up with a false alarm. Daddy usually shut the alarm off when that happened.

Our neighbors had to put up with the false alarms, too. They did not like it. Usually by the time the alarm got shut off, lots of our neighbors had stopped by to visit and find out why our house was making all that noise.

One day, though, Mommy was home alone when the alarm went off. Daddy was not there to shut it off, and the neighbors no longer seemed to care about the noise — or were to busy to come visit.

So, Mommy told us to stay in the living room, and she went to check out the apartment. To get there, she went up our stairs, across the attic, and down into the apartment on the other side of the building. Whew! No one was there. Once again, it was a false alarm. She turned off the alarm.

The police were already on the way, unfortunately. They had heard the alarm, too. They walked into the house just as Mommy was walking down the stairs. She stopped to talk to them. Standing on the third stair up, she was the same height as the police officer who had entered our house. (Either Mommy is not very tall, or the police officer *was* very tall.)

"We heard the alarm, ma'am," the police officer said.

"Oh, there's nothing to worry about," Mommy reassured him. "I just checked, and it is a false alarm."

The police officer looked Mommy up and down. Obviously, he thought that Mommy was not very tall because he asked her, "And just what did a little thing like you think you were going to do if you found someone there?"

Actually, Mommy had not really considered that, but she thought quickly and allowed that she could chew an intruder off at the knees. The police officer did not think that was a very good answer, but I know that Mommy could have done it (especially if she were wearing her combat boots).

Conclusion:
No one should underestimate the fierceness of a mommy.

Thinking Literally

Understanding things literally is something that Mr. Spock on *Star Trek* does. It is also something that my mommy does. I do not know if it is because she is a detail-oblivious type or if there is another reason. Anyway, that's probably why she is gullible and why she drove the deuce-and-a-half.

Apparently, she has always taken things literally. At least, that's what my aunts and uncles tell me. I can give you an example of that, too.

When she was a little girl, according to my grown-up relatives, she was very active in a number of youth organizations. One of those was the Junior Grange. The Junior Grange is for kids up to age 16, when they can join the regular Grange. It is mostly found in small towns and rural areas.

When Mommy was ten, she was Master of the Junior Grange. That is the highest office there is. As Master, she had to lead the meetings.

That year, my mommy's Junior Grange was voted as the best in the state. That meant, that all the officers had to go the state capitol to the New Hampshire State Grange meeting and put on the "degree," a special kind of meeting. Mommy and her friends did that. There were lots of really important people at the New Hampshire State Grange meeting.

At the end of the meeting, the matron—that is the adult person who acts as an advisor to the Junior Grange members— told Mommy that she should now have some of the bigwigs speak.

Mommy did not understand what bigwigs were. Mommy had never been out of the Maine-New Hampshire area, but she did a lot of reading, and she knew that there were all kinds of different groups of people in the world. So, instead of thinking that the matron was speaking figuratively, she took her literally, assuming that there was a special group of people called bigwigs.

"Would any bigwigs in the room like to speak?" asked Mommy. The matron looked very embarrassed, and no one stood up to speak. They said that the year Mommy presided over the degree was the only year that no one spoke at the joint New Hampshire State Grange-Junior Grange meeting.

Conclusion:
Sometimes asking is better than assuming.

Typing Typos

I know that Mommy would not make a very good secretary because I have seen her typing. Actually, her typing is pretty good, but she makes mistakes sometimes that are very funny. Well, I think they are funny, but the people she types them for do not.

One of the words she has trouble with is *public*. She keeps forgetting to type the letter "l" into the word. For example, one time her book publisher called her at the last minute. The publisher was laughing, but she wanted Mommy to make a change real fast. Instead of "public events," Mommy had typed "pubic events."

Daddy knows what that mistake is like. Once Mommy typed his resume, and he distributed it all over Pittsburgh. He stopped sending it out, however, when he got a call from one potential employer. Mommy had typed that Daddy had "extensive experience in pubic relations." Daddy types his own resumes now.

One time Mommy applied for a grant to go to Siberia. She wanted Daddy and us to go with her. She typed in the application the information that Daddy and all of us kinds wanted to go with her, if possible

When she was interviewed for the grant, one of the interviewers asked her if she thought that Daddy should go to Russia with her, given his problem and the nature of Russian society. Mommy did not understand. The interviewer did not want to spell things out.

"Well, you know, the problem you mention in the application," he said.

Mommy still did not understand.

"Well, you know that in Russia people drink a lot more than in the United States," the interviewer explained. "So do you really think it is wise to take your husband, with his problem, with you?"

"What problem?" Mommy demanded to know. She was really confused.

"This one," the interviewer responded, He handed her application to her and pointed out what she had typed: "Souse and children will accompany me."

Daddy won't let Mommy type anything anymore. I think he made the right decision. And I know what to get Mommy for Christmas: typing lessons.

Conclusion:
Only some people can be secretaries;
others should let the secretaries do their typing work.

Mommy and the Priest

No detail-oblivious type of person can make it through life without a bit of sacrilege if Mommy is an example. At one point, Mommy was drawn into activities connected with the Russian Orthodox Church. They were helping her with an Orthodox child whom she was trying to help. For that reason, she sometimes had to go to the church, and sometimes she had to talk to people at the church. Once she had to talk to the priest.

The priest walked up to Mommy and held out his hand. His hand had a really big ring on it. Mommy did notice the ring—it was impossible not to miss it—but thought no more about it. Being very polite, Mommy took the priest's hand and shook it energetically. (She had been told that one should have a firm handshake, and she does. The priest now knows that, too.)

Obviously, the advice about firm handshakes was not meant for all situations. Mommy understood from the shocked looks all around, beginning with the priest's face, that she was not supposed to have done that. So what was she supposed to have done?

Mommy was confused. She reached into her childhood memories, got as close to a history of details as a detail-oblivious type could, and pulled out an image of school. She remembered some training in deportment in second grade. It had been a long time since she had practiced doing it, but just in case it was the proper thing to do, Mommy curtsied.

Everyone laughed. Mommy was embarrassed, but she still

did not know what she should do or should have done.

Someone whispered to Mommy that she was supposed to kiss the priest's ring. However, he had already put his hand down by his side. Mommy figured it was better to leave bad enough alone. She figured that she would have looked even sillier crawling onto the floor to kiss his ring.

Conclusion:
Not everything you need to know gets learned in kindergarten.

Life in Cyberspace

My sister writes to my mommy a lot in cyberspace. We all do. One time, however, my sister wanted to send Mommy a package. She did not know where to send it. She could not send it to cyberspace! I think she had a problem sending a package to cyberspace because there was no zip code to use. All real places have zip codes, right? So cyberspace must not be a real place, at least the way I figure.

Mommy lives in cyberspace for a couple of reasons. First, she travels a lot, and that is the way she keeps in touch with us. (I have a place in cyberspace, too. You can write to me there at CBLeaver@yahoo.com.) Second, sometimes Mommy's work requires her to be in cyberspace.

For several years, Mommy worked for an organization that existed primarily in cyberspace. People in a number of cities across America worked from home, and they were linked by e-mail. Mommy did many different things for that organization. Sometimes she would send out addresses for people helping with specific projects.

Mommy learned the importance of accurate typing (although she probably will never be able to type accurately without those typing lessons I plan to get for her), when she received a number of surprised responses from her message giving the address of Mr. and Mrs. Lord. Mommy had titled the message: "The Lord's E-Mail Address." Everyone thought that Mommy had some great connections.

Another time Mommy had to answer a letter from a lady named Fatema. She wrote, "Hi Fatema." The computer spell checker did not recognize the name, Fatema, so it corrected it to the closest thing. Mommy had the automatic correction on, and she did not notice until after the letter was sent how the computer had corrected her typing. She was very embarrassed when she saw that her letter, already sent, said, "Hi Fatty."

Conclusion:
Double-check the typing whether or not you did it yourself.

Moldovan Roulette

My cybermom sometimes relies too much on e-mail. Well, actually, it is not that she relies on it too much. It is that she trusts it. At least, she used to trust it. I think she has learned not to trust it anymore. Her trust was definitely broken in Moldova.

There she was teaching a seminar and keeping in touch with people back home, as usual, via e-mail. One day she had a number of letters to answer, and she did that very quickly. However, somehow the mail went to all the wrong people. Mommy found this out when people sent her very puzzled responses; they did not know that the mail had gone to the wrong addresses because Mommy does not often use names in salutations. Here are some examples:

She sent a note to my sister who was moving to Illinois to go to school. She wrote a very simple, quick note, "I will give you $1000 to move to Illinois." The note went instead to a friend of Mommy's. The friend said that she would be willing to take the money, but she wanted to know why Mommy wanted her to move to Illinois.

Mommy sent a note to my other sister, who was living with my older sister and not behaving very well. Mommy was very succinct: "Either get your act together or move in with me!" That note, by accident, went to a colleague Mommy had just met at the State Department. She was quite surprised by it!

Daddy got a note that was supposed to go to a college professor. He was very confused. He did not understand what it was that Mommy wanted him to do.

Mommy sent a lovey-dovey note to Daddy. She did use the salutation then, but it went to a high-ranking official with whom she was supposed to meet when she got back to the United States—and that guy had the same first name as Daddy!

What was it that Murphy said? "If something can go wrong, it will." Mommy says that Murphy lives with us.

Conclusion:
Those who live with Murphy should not tempt fate.

The End

Well, that's what life with Mommy is like. Thanks for letting me share that with you. Next time, I'll tell you all about Daddy.

'Bye.

CB

Shenan (CB) Leaver (with Betty Lou Leaver)

ABOUT THE
AUTHORS

Shenan (CB) Leaver (with Betty Lou Leaver)

CB Leaver

Shenan Leaver, better known as CB, was born in Pittsburgh, in 1979. Due on Christmas Day, he decided to arrive considerably earlier—November 11—and started his entrance into the world while his mommy was teaching a university class. He has been doing things his own way ever since.

He is a 1998 graduate of Hayes High School in Delaware, Ohio. The youngest of four siblings, he has attended schools in four different states (Pennsylvania, Virginia, California, and Ohio), where he has met many different kinds of people and they have met him.

Until recently, he worked full-time at HOPE of Monterey County. While there, he gave new meaning to the word and name.

Now living independently on the Arroyo Seco River, in the woods and mountains near the Ventana Wilderness Area, he likes traipsing across the river on a swinging bridge to catch a bus to go to work in Soledad or to church in Greenfield. He tells his many friends in these places stories about his mommy—and his daddy and his siblings.

CB is working on a new book. It is called *Daddy Called the Cops on Mommy*. He hopes you will read that book, too, once he finishes it.

Betty Lou Leaver

Betty Lou (Ham) Leaver is CB's Mommy. Who and what she is has already been related in more than sufficient detail on the pages within this book.